Other books by this author:

CAPPAWHITE

# BEYOND THE FOREST'S EDGE

## CAPPAWHITE II

## GERALD J. TATE

The Derwent Press
Derbyshire, England

www.derwentpress.com

# BEYOND THE FOREST'S EDGE
## CAPPAWHITE II
by
### Gerald J. Tate

ISBN 10: 1-84667-027-6
ISBN 13: 978-1-84667-027-5

Cover art and book design by:
Pam Marin-Kingsley, www.far-angel.com

by
The Derwent Press
Derbyshire, England
www.derwentpress.com

In memory of my good friend,

Big Bill

1957-1988

Special thanks to

Chuck, Nick, Jake,
Davey,  Steve and Michael,
who all helped
and encouraged me along the way.

*Down in the forest, where no one can see*

*Alone in the darkness, she waits there for me.*

*Her wailing brings forth, the final death knell,*

*This collector of souls, this demon from hell.*

# CHAPTER 1

## LOS ANGELES 2003

There had been no mourners at the open grave as they lowered the casket slowly down into the cold earth. Just professional men, paid to do a job. The priest had said a quick prayer, and then it was over. The darkening clouds overhead and the cold, almost gale force wind, made the undertakers glad it had been a quick and short service.

Nelson, the head gravedigger, clumsily pulled out the little hip flask from his back pocket and took a sly swig. Then, he awkwardly pushed the tarpaulin over the narrow opening, and disrespectfully kicked the lone wreath out onto the edge of the pathway. The drink he had consumed the previous night, had not agreed with him, and the piercing headache he had experienced so many times before, pulsated in every crevice of the angry man's skull.

"Damn," Nelson muttered, as he checked his watch and tapped at it roughly with his bloated fingers. This would be a long day.

Then he yawned loudly, and rubbed at his greasy forehead with a soiled handkerchief, before slowly making his way back to the office. He would finish with the grave later.

The old woman had left all her worldly goods to the little mission store on the corner, and a surprisingly sizable bank account had been donated to the church. The only luxury she had allowed herself was to pay for a top of the line, solid oak coffin, with gold-plated handles and nameplate. The wreath had also been paid for by the old woman, long before she died. "To keep things respectable," she had said.

Even the little poem affixed to the wreath on a white card had been written by her:

Oh take me, Lord,
to Thine wondrous bosom
where untold knowledge
does there abound.
Feed me with divine salvation,
Take my hand and keep me sound.

Sarah Tweedy

As the last vehicle drove out through the gates of the cemetery on that wet, windy day, a lone figure stared out across the headstones. No one could see it, its face hidden deep within its hood, but it was there, blackened in the shadows.

Somewhere amongst the swaying branches it lurked, just outside, beyond the cemetery wall, alone. Even the birds, their primitive instincts alerted, stayed clear, refusing to fly within fifty feet of this frightening presence. It was still watching when the dark came to claim the last beads of light, as the day slowly surrendered to night. Its mouth opened slightly, twisted and stretched. Then it hissed loudly.

It was ready!

But it felt a fear. A fear so great, that it almost turned away. This place was not where it should be, it knew. Something dangerous was all around, and only some inner madness was keeping it there.

Nelson pulled on his heavy coat, rather clumsily, and grumbled loudly as he removed the large heavy padlock from the metal cabinet. He had shared the house at the edge of the cemetery this last four months with old Patterson, the caretaker. The job of locking the gates usually belonged to Patterson, but his brother had suffered a bad stroke earlier in the day. Nelson had told him he would take care of locking the gates that night, while Patterson went to the hospital to visit his brother. Now he was almost sorry he had suggested it, because he had secretly hoped Patterson would return in time to take over again. As he padlocked the solid iron gates, a heavy squall of rain blew into his face and he cursed loudly. Then as he made his way back to the house he saw something. A movement! Just at the point where the trees started, outside the cemetery wall. Right dab centre in the middle of a group of cedar trees.

Normally Nelson would have put this down to his over active imagination. But not this time! He knew who it was. It was those damned hoodlums again. Those good for nuthin,' sawed-off pieces of cow shit who had been breaking into the cemetery at night. Five times in the last three months they had done it—having their fucking weed and booze parties up by the crematorium. Those useless cops had been called numerous times and still no one had been caught. It was the mess they always left afterward that cut it for Nelson. Beer bottles, broken glass and filthy habits strewn just about everywhere. It was normally Patterson's job to clean up their mess. Now though, he knew that if Patterson didn't return tonight, he would have to clean up their goddamn mess tomorrow himself.

Well, as far as Nelson was concerned, there wasn't a rat's ass chance that this was going to happen, and he quickly and purposely entered the house. *These punks weren't dealing with some old asshole now,* he thought. *Patterson may not be able to do anything about you, you shit heads. But I sure in God's name can.*

Nelson almost wrenched the door off the large walk in cupboard. He hurriedly grabbed the flashlight, and searched around. Then his eyes lit up as he saw what he wanted.

"Matilda," he said aloud, as if the old baseball bat could hear him. "Let's do us some punk bashing!"

Nelson slipped from the house and quickly moved out through a small side gate. As he silently crept along the outside wall of the graveyard, he kept the flashlight turned off, tapping the bat off the back of his leg as he went. Even though it was dark, he could clearly see the figure in the branches, hiding.

Nelson didn't even notice the rain blowing into his face, because his mind was occupied with one thing only, to crack a few heads, and finish these break-ins once and for all. He would feel immensely proud, telling old Patterson of how he alone, had solved the problem. He hadn't checked the flashlight, but instinctively knew it would work. Old Patterson was always very meticulous with all of their gear, making sure they were serviced, and regularly—cleaning every damn thing there was around the place. Always new batteries when needed.

Nelson flicked the switch and the flashlight burst into life, just as he knew it would, and he shone it up into the tree. "What in Gods name?" he whispered.

A large hooded figure came into view. It sat with its back to him, unmoving.

Nelson roughly pulled at the branches, and for a man of his size and weight, surprisingly climbed up onto the thickest of them with great ease. A branch flew back and hit him hard, full on the face, almost knocking him from the tree. But he held on tightly. Then he kissed Matilda and violently poked it into the back of the hooded figures head, sword thrust fashion.

"Want some of this, you shit head?" the angry man roared above the high, almost deafening wind. "Come outa there, you bastard."

Yet, the creature remained still, hardly noticing him as it struggled with what it had to do next.

"Why, it's only a dummy," Nelson moaned, as he reached to pull the hood off. But then he paused and cracked it once more in the head, but much harder this time. *Just to be sure,* he thought.

Still the creature didn't move.

Then Nelson positioned himself so that he could get a real good swipe at it, and let fly.

*CE-rackkk*! Matilda sounded, as she clunked heavily into its head.

"Why those cheap no good punks," Nelson complained. "Why they've left me a goddamn dum..."

Suddenly it spun around, and he dropped Matilda to the ground. It was staring into his face now. The rows of black pointed teeth and the yellow snake like tongue crashed into his face before he could think another thought. No one could hear him scream, as his lifeless, decapitated body was thrown from the tree. His bloodied head impaled onto a sharp branch.

Then suddenly in the darkness, it moved out from the tree, and with great speed. Over the wall it went, hovering, quickly passing through the headstones, toward old Sarah Tweedy's, grave.

Its head convulsed violently, as its body shuddered. The creature somehow knew the consequences of moving onto a place like this. The dangers to it and its kind, but it was desperate, and it pushed these feelings of fear from its being. The rows of black pointed, rotted teeth chattered, as it moved across the consecrated ground. Flesh ripped from its face, arms, legs and back, and the creature screamed in pain. It dropped to the ground and fell heavily against the headstones, smashing them, leaving piles of torn and broken marble in its wake. But still, on it came, as it pounded its way toward the old woman's final resting place.

Then the creature flung itself headlong into the freshly cut grave, tearing at the clay walls on either side. Its long fingers ripped out large chunks of earth and stone that showered down with a dull thud as they peppered the large wooden casket below.

It snarled as it gripped the casket in its strong spindly hands, and wrenched it up from the grave's floor, tearing off the gold-plated ornamental handles as it flung the heavy oak coffin up into the air and out from the narrow opening. The heavy casket cracked and split, landing with a loud crunch, before finally resting on its side.

The beast shrieked and wailed as it felt the power of some unknown force rip and tear at it. Still it fought on, unrelenting, as it felt a thousand daggers stab at its body. It lurched violently, headlong to the ground, stumbling and crashing in all directions, screaming to the heavens. Its aim to get at the old woman was paramount though, as it struggled back over to the heavy oak coffin. Then it tore at the casket's top panel, ripping it from its hinges, before throwing the lid far into the trees.

For a brief moment the creature stared down, almost as if in prayer, at the peaceful, dead woman. Then it roughly pulled her from the casket and floated high into the night sky, the old woman's body held tightly in its arms. Its cape strained hard in the strong, increasing winds, as it disappeared up into the clouds, wailing.

# CHAPTER 2

Dan Winters pulled his VW Beetle into the already crowded car park and cursed his luck. Beatrice had kept him late for work again. Poor neurotic Beatrice, was a woman whose love for her mother was paramount over everyone and everything else. She had cursed him, threatened him, and even blamed him. But he had stuck to his guns, and now it had all gone pear-shaped.

His mind wandered back to all those many weeks ago when they had first driven to the old folk's home, with its beautiful gardens of palm-trees and the ornamental birds strategically placed everywhere.

*A smell of lavender had hung heavily in the air, giving the place an almost oriental feel, and Dan breathed in hard, filling his lungs with the pleasant aroma.*

*Then they met the welcoming staff, a surprisingly young staff that seemed as if nothing was too much trouble for them. Beatrice had seemed fine at the time, talking and joking with the head care nurse who ensured her that her mother would get the best treatment possible.*

*But at the swanky restaurant on the return journey she had refused to speak a word, pointing at the menu to the waitress as though she were a deaf mute.*

*'What in Gods name are you doing? What the hell's wrong with you?' Dan whispered angrily to her, puzzled at his wife's strange behaviour.*

*Beatrice sat in silence for a full minute, tears welling up in her eyes before she spoke. 'Bastard!' she yelled into his face, causing everyone in the packed restaurant to look around at them.*

*Dan felt himself flush with a mixture of embarrassment and anger, confused at what she was doing.*

*'This bastard made me put my mother in the old folk's home,' she sobbed to everyone and anyone who would listen. Beatrice had never sworn at him like this before.*

*And now! Well what a time and goddamn place to do it, he thought.*

*Suddenly the tall head waiter appeared at their table, his nervous but polite smile, and his bow tie that projected an air of authority, somehow seemed menacing to Dan.*

*'I'm sorry Sir, Madam, but I'm afraid I must ask you to leave,' he said politely.*

*'Why?' Dan asked, angrily.*

*The tall waiter did not answer, but simply stood to attention like a soldier on parade, and pointed toward the door. Dan rose slowly from his seat, and then quickly made his way through the gauntlet of stares, uncaring if Beatrice was behind him now or not. He could feel the silence coming from every table, the piercing eyes glued to him, watching his every move. This was like some strange nightmare. How in Gods name could she do this to him? After everything he had done for her. Worked his ass off to keep them. How could she shame him like this? Suddenly the door felt a hell of a way further off than it did when they had first entered the restaurant. And still the faces stared at him.*

*Dan stopped for a second and glared around at them. 'My wife, she's not feeling so good,' he moaned, mumbling his excuse to no one in particular, before moving quickly to the door.*

*As he reached the exit, the head waiter was directly behind him, and he could hear Beatrice sobbing loudly as she closely followed the waiter like some grovelling, obedient pet.*

*'Goodnight Sir, Madam,' said the waiter, and Dan thought he detected a smirk.*

*'Yeah, fuck you too pal,' Dan said, and walked briskly to the car. Then he paused and doubled back, his face like thunder. He marched past Beatrice and pushed violently at the restaurant door. The headwaiter turned instinctively, his posture unchanging, and Dan raised his fist. Suddenly the headwaiter was no longer standing upright, but cowering down foetus like, into the corner, his hands covering his face.*

'*Please don't hit me,*' *he begged as Dan moved in close.*

'*You smug piece of shit,*' *Dan shouted.* '*By the time I'm finished with you, you'll be eating your dinner through a fucking straw.*' *Then Dan looked up, and those same wide-eyed faces were still staring.*

'*Someone send for the police,*' *a voice said, and Dan quickly walked away, now feeling more embarrassed over his vacant threat than the incident itself.*

*As he was about to drive off he turned around and pointed menacingly at Beatrice, who had decided to sit in the rear seat of the car, away from him.*

'*Never ever do that again,*' *Dan warned as Beatrice, head in her hands, ignored him.*

*He didn't notice how the light drizzling rain had penetrated his hair and shoulders, running down his rugged face like little beads of sweat, and as he drove off he roughly swiped at his grey, receding hairline.*

*Then as they had neared home, Dan thought about an article he had written in his column about domestic disputes and how a poor woman had almost been beaten to death by her monster of a husband. He turned and looked at the still sobbing Beatrice, and he realised how close he had become to being that monster himself. A feeling of guilt rose over him.*

*Dan knew that he could have tried harder to bring her mother home to live with them, and make some sort of compromise. Yet, he also knew the consequences of what this would mean to them.*

*The damn woman's mind had almost gone, and she would do things. And at seventy years of age, parading naked in front of everyone (which was what she had been doing lately) was not something he wanted to witness. This, and her obsession with matches and cigarette lighters, also made her a damn dangerous person to have around.*

*Then there was the urinating all around her house, he thought. Why her home smelt like a goddamn ammonia factory, a place Dan avoided like the plague. Anyway, they had talked it over, agreeing that this was the only way. He thought Beatrice had listened to reason, but now he had to put up with her worsening, erratic behaviour.*

*Then there was the job issue. Dan had recently been hauled in to face his boss at the paper, only to be told his work was getting stale. It wasn't exactly put to him like that, but he got the message. It was also clear to him that it was all Beatrice's fault.*

Dan pulled the VW part way up onto the grass verge as the rain whipped heavily around the windows. He was aware of the large security camera pointing directly at him, but he parked the car anyway, ignoring it. At least he would be close to the main entrance. He pulled up his collar and ran through the biting wind and rain, briefcase in hand. Then he was through the tall revolving doors and into the spacious, welcoming hallway.

Jackson, the large bear-like security guard, quickly approached Dan and called to him. He had been caught in a parking indiscretion, and now he would have to walk back through the heavy rain and re-park his car.

He was just about to make some feeble excuse, when Jackson spoke first.

"Letter here for you Mr Winters, hand-delivered this morning. Signed for it myself," Jackson grinned.

Dan quickly snatched the large pink envelope from Jackson's hand and walked on. "Signed for it myself," he lowly mumbled, mimicking Jackson. He didn't seem to realise that Jackson could hear him as he hurried inside the elevator.

Jackson shook his head and stared into space for a moment, before slowly walking back to his post. Jackson had, up until that point, always liked Dan. He had thought of him as a polite, friendly, open-minded sort of guy. But lately, Jackson noticed Dan had seemed withdrawn and unfriendly. Jackson knew there was a reason for this sort of behaviour though, there always was. He had witnessed it first hand, in Nam, and now his mind wandered back to those times.

*He was a young twenty-five year-old then, but he had already been a Sergeant for almost two of them. Jackson had been there in 1968 when his comrades had wiped out all of the people in the village of My Lai. Over three hundred, men, Women and children had been killed and raped*

*that day. He had shot a girl through the temple as she had tried to run away. But only God and he knew that when he pulled the trigger, he thought he was killing a man. Afterward, when Jackson viewed her body, he witnessed a sight that would haunt him for the rest of his life.*

*A young girl, probably no more than sixteen years old, he felt. A beautiful young girl, who under different circumstances and given the opportunity, could have graced the catwalk of any modelling show, anywhere in the world. Instead, here she was, lying sprawled on her back in the dirt, with her brains blasted out around her skull. And he did it!*

*'Awe, come off it, Sarge. It's only a gook,' Felix, the corporal had said to him, as Jackson threw up five feet from her body and cried.*

*An old woman wailed somewhere in the background, before a shot silenced her also. Jackson didn't remember punching Felix afterward, but then that was just what the day was like—a crazy, mixed up sort of fucking day.*

*Anyway, it's done and dusted, he thought. That damned war, which made punks into men, and men into punks.*

Even at sixty years of age, Jackson could never get that little girl out of his head.

"Ask not what your country can do for you," he said to the fresh-faced kid, who had been following him about like a puppy dog, and who had only been on the job for two days. The kid's uniform looked two sizes too big for him as it hung loosely from his shoulders.

Jackson would be retiring in six days, and he had planned to tell Dan about it, say goodbye, and shake the man's hand kind of thing. Now though, he would say nothing.

As Dan sipped his morning coffee he looked for the letter opener that was buried beneath the mountain of reports, folders, books, and every other item that had piled up on his desk, stuff that he had accumulated over a long period of time.

"Gotta get you sorted out sometime soon," he said to the unsightly pile as if it could understand him.

After a moment he roughly ripped open the pink envelope and stared at the neatly written bundle of pages. He propped his feet up onto the desk and began to read.

Dear Mr Winters:

My name is Sarah Tweedy, and if you're reading this then I am already dead. I have left instructions that you were to be given this letter immediately after my burial, so I have just recently departed from this cruel world. I was over seventy-five years old, but I always read your column. It's because of the *trust I feel for you that I have written to you now. I do not write this letter easily, but I need your help.*

*You see, I just don't know what is going to happen to my husband now that I'm gone, or rather, the thing that my husband has become since his death, thirty-five years ago, and...*

Dan threw his feet from the desk and sprang upright in his chair, pulling the letter tightly to his face. "The thing my husband has become since his death, thirty five years ago" he read aloud, and laughed. "Jeez mother, what fucking psycho sick ward did you spring up from?"

Dan sat the letter down onto the top of the computer monitor, which was the only free space he could find, and left the office. He had a story to cover about a Hell's Angel's conference in LA, and he would need to pull out all the stops to get it filed away in time.

"Did you get me that info, Bennett?" Dan asked the young apprentice journalist, who was sitting daydreaming in the corner.

"Sure thing, Mr Winters. I have it here. I didn't wanna leave it in your office though—I thought it might get lost," he said sarcastically, and giggled.

"Damn, smart ass kid," laughed Rodgers, the janitor, as he walked past.

"Yeah, too fucking smart," answered Dan. "Watch it, kid." He shook a finger at the laughing Bennett and snatched the folder from the boy's hand. Then he held his hand up in a backhand motion, pretending he was going to strike the boy.

It was still pouring with rain when Dan turned out onto the interstate, and he pushed hard on the gas. He was sure Beatrice would be in a state when he got home, the way she always was. But no matter, he would just have to put up with it—at least until she came to her senses.

Dan could never get to the bottom of Beatrice's problems; never get too close before she would push him away. His love life was practically non-existent, and as for any affection shown on her part, well, he felt would have more luck cuddling up to a rattlesnake. But he had made this bed for himself, and he would just have to sleep in it.

Dan's thoughts then turned once more to Sarah Tweedy's letter. Something was familiar here. *Sarah Tweedy*, he thought to himself. He was sure he had heard that name somewhere before.

"Sarah Tweedy, Sarah Tweedy," he repeated aloud as he searched his memory for some sort of recollection.

Dan then turned the car radio on and the voice of the newsreader was babbling on about Senator Bell.

"Senator Bell, a fine man of strong family values. And a man who could make America great again, given the chance," the newsreader said.

This same Senator and "man of strong family values" that Dan knew to be a serial cheat. He had run the story about Bell past his boss, along with the details of how Bell was screwing his secretary, as well as two other women. These spurned women had come forward to warn every other woman in America about the guy.

*Of course, the fact they were being paid money by the paper to reveal all, and come clean about the sex-crazed congressman would play a very small part in the equation*, he thought, and smirked as he remembered how the woman had badgered him to say they weren't being paid for their story. *Everyone nowadays just wants a quick buck.*

Dan had worked hard, both day and night, on the story though, and tied up all the loose ends. The story was big and ready to break. Then two days later, he was told to drop the story. "It's too dangerous and not in the public's best interest," he had been told.

*Why this piece of sleaze carried more weight than the freekin' president?* Dan had thought at the time. Thinking about it now though, he realised that this was about the time his career had started taking a nose dive, and was still going under.

Maybe it wasn't the stress of Beatrice that had caused his decline at the newspaper after all, but the long reaching arms of the mysterious men in black. Those government men that everyone knows exist, but no one ever gets to see. Then the president's voice came over the air, talking about the deepening crisis in Iraq...

"Good old George W Hackenabush, always there when you need a goddamn freekin invasion," Dan moaned at the radio set. Then Senator Bell's voice rang out again, and Dan thumped the radio in despair.

Entering the driveway, Dan paused for a moment before getting out of the car. He looked up into the darkening sky, and then pulled slowly at the door.

It would have been easy for him to stay in the car and drive away. Drive somewhere across the vast country, hundreds or even thousands of miles away from all of his problems, never again to return. But deep down Dan knew that Beatrice needed him more than she could ever imagine, or admit to. No, he would not desert her.

Beatrice sat in silence as he entered the room, and fiddled with her thumbs. "I want a divorce," she said quietly.

Dan had now lost count of the times she had asked him this. It had become part of the every day evening ritual. As usual, he ignored her and moved to the kitchen to prepare them something to eat.

Later that evening, Dan flicked on the news channel and listened as the gory details of another gangland killing echoed out from the screen. Another guy bludgeoned and stabbed to death in broad daylight on the street corner. Had his throat almost torn out.

"Jesus Christ, Sarah Tweedy!" he shouted, frightening Beatrice, as he jumped up from his seat, spilling the can of Bud he had been drinking all over his trousers. He had covered a gangland slaying about four or five years before this. The guy had his fucking head ripped off in an old woman's apartment. *Sarah Tweedy's apartment*, he remembered.

Sarah had said then that she hadn't seen anything, and the police finally put the killing into the cold case files as "unsolved." In an interview, sometime later, the old woman had told Dan that she was asleep when the guy was killed. Yet for some reason, Dan didn't believe her. When he pushed her for more details however, the old lady told him to go ask her husband. The husband had just happened to be dead—for about thirty years. So, Dan had let it go, thinking she had lost her marbles.

Now this same old woman had written to him. "Sarah Tweedy," he said aloud again.

Beatrice continued to ignore him. Now she couldn't even stand the sound of his voice. There was nothing left, she felt, and she turned her back to him.

Dan resumed his thoughts; unaware of the ever increasing hatred Beatrice was building up for him.

At the time of the killing in old Sarah's apartment, he had felt that the police had been hiding something. The Sergeant had seemed nervous and agitated, cursing and swearing at anyone below him in the chain of command.

*Yes,* Dan thought. *This case always stank to the high heavens.* He threw his empty Bud into the waste basket, and turned toward Beatrice.

"Goodnight, honey," he said, as he leaned across and kissed her cheek.

Beatrice responded by grabbing a tissue from a box on the coffee table, and vigorously rubbed at the side of her face until it turned red.

Later as he lay in bed alone, Dan wondered how things would have turned out for him if Lynn hadn't died in the accident all those years ago.

*Beautiful Lynn,* Dan thought, *who was always smiling. He had loved her, loved her deeply and completely.* They had only been married for six months when it happened. Lynn had offered to cover another shift for one of the nurses at the hospital. That was just the sort of caring person she was, even though she was four months pregnant. She had promised to take it easy, and cut back on her hours. But then Lynn would always be the one to put other people first.

The truck that crushed her car had so many defective parts that it would have taken weeks to write them all down. The immigrant driving it could hardly speak a word of English, and Dan soon found out that his driving documents were as illegal as the stolen license plates on his truck.

But it had happened, and he had lost Lynn and the baby. Dan had gotten over it—to a point, over the years. Yet, he felt sometimes that he had only married Beatrice on some sort of damn rebound. He had never loved Beatrice the way he had loved Lynn, even though they had been married now for much longer.

Dan sometimes felt guilty for feeling this way, but this was the way it was and had to be. He always knew though, that if there were a way to get Lynn back, he would take her. He fantasized that maybe

Lynn hadn't died, but had been kidnapped by some Mafia boss, or taken by an Arab prince who would finally tire of her, and then finally let her go.

Dan knew he would leave Beatrice at the drop of a hat, if this were so—but the reality of it was that he had seen Lynn in the coffin, through his bloodshot eyes. Watched as they lowered her into the cold ground, and he knew she wasn't coming back, ever.

*Death has that terrible finality about it,* he thought. *Those things you so much wanted to say to someone, but never got around to, or simply forgot.* Now Dan had a million things he needed to say to Lynn, but never would. He thought about how the baby would have looked, had it been born. Lynn had already picked the names, "Grace" for a girl and "Tom," should it be a boy. It was all Lynn had talked about since she had found out she was pregnant. She had even planned out a play room in bright, multi-colours, with a plastic slide and swing.

For a moment, Dan pictured her and the baby playing and holding hands together in God's heaven. They were laughing and Lynn was singing. She had always sang to him with her beautiful voice, which could have graced any choir.

Dan wiped away a little tear. He pulled the covers half over his face, and stared hard at the ceiling, before saying a silent prayer for Lynn and the baby. He wished more than anything that he could be with them. Join them somehow and be happy. It was a notion he had dangerously, and seriously thought about many times before.

Finally, sleep came to claim him.

# CHAPTER 3

## CAPPAWHITE, IRELAND

Connor lay awake and struggled in the darkness to read the face of the large grandfather clock that was propped into the far corner of the room. It had been his mother's clock, and was now his, handed down through the family from generation to generation. The clock's sentimental value was worth much more than the bedraggled timepiece itself, which would need much attention and money spent to bring it back to its former glory.

*Three o-bloody clock*, he thought, as he pulled the large duvet over his head. It was the thought of all the work they still had to do at the old house, and the budgeting that had kept him awake.

Carol had worked out the costs of renovating the old house, and the eight en-suite guest rooms that they had agreed on, were to be set to the very highest standard possible. But now they were over budget by twenty thousand big ones, and six week's behind schedule. With just two months left before the holiday season starting, and with their guest house already pre-booked, things would have to start happening, and soon.

Connor would often go into the other rooms at night, and pace the floor with the worry of it all. But he tried not to show it in front of Carol, although he knew that she, too, was having a hard time over the setbacks and trouble.

Connor pulled himself up from the bed and made his way, barefoot to the kitchen, yawning as he went. The kitchen hallway was filled with building supplies. He cursed as he stepped on something sharp.

**A piece of mortar or some debris from those bloody, lazy workmen,** he supposed.

In a tired haze, Connor made himself a cup of tea. As he walked back into the spacious living room, he suddenly looked toward the door, and felt uneasy. He then looked away, to the plasma –screen television, shuddering at his reflection in the dark empty screen.

*God, am I really as thin as that?* he thought, now noticing that his weight loss seemed to be getting even worse. Stress could be one reason, but the doctor said he would have to come in for some tests. *Tests,* he thought suspiciously, *What sort of bloody tests?*

"I know what tests," Connor said aloud. "Bloody cancer tests, that's what."

*They can't fool me with all their medical jargon and fancy talk,* he thought. Then Connor looked toward the door again and his hair on the back of his neck stood on end. *What the hell is wrong with me tonight?*

Connor moved slowly to the door, stopping to take a sip of tea on the way. He leaned down and quickly looked through the little peep hole in the door. He somehow felt foolish. Alright, he had heard the stories about the place when Mrs Doyle once owned it. But even Carol had laughed them off, and told him to go get a life when he had mentioned the subject—which made him feel even more foolish now.

The horrifying stories the superstitious villagers had been spreading over the years about the house had done them no harm in the buying of the place though. No one wanted this secluded, run down house with all the rumours of demons haunting it. So the price of the house had fallen to half its normal worth, and they had purchased the huge structure for a song.

Connor tried to focus through the peephole, but suddenly jumped back when he saw something. He dropped the cup, and spilled the hot tea on his legs, but he made no sound as he slowly backed towards the bedroom. He couldn't take his eyes off the door.

There had been a large hooded monk standing outside, about ten feet from the door. Its arms were folded and its dark head bowed, as if in prayer.

"Police!" Carol heard Connor muffle into the phone, and she sprang from the bed.

"What are you bloody doing, Connor?" she asked, puzzled.

"There's someone outside the door, dressed as a damn monk," he whispered frantically, unable to hide the fear in his voice.

"Well you can't phone the police, he hasn't done anything," she argued.

"Its three o'clock in the bloody morning, and he's on our property. What do you think he's doing, having a fucking picnic?" Connor hissed.

Carol walked to the door and looked through the peep hole, but could see nothing.

"Hello! Yes, police," she heard Connor say in the background.

*When I got Connor,* she thought, *I really picked the runt of the litter.* He was always one to run and panic at the slightest thing, leaving her to sort out all of their over stretched problems. *Always a bloody whiner,* she thought.

Carol would have left him if she could, but now her money was tied up in this house and for the time being she was stuck with him. She would have been much happier with Andrew, and she knew that, but it was too late now. Andrew had married, and gone to Scotland to live with Julie Hutton. Bloody Julie four eyes Hutton, who at school couldn't even get a boy to look sideways at her, but who had run off with the only man Carol had ever loved.

"There's no one there," Carol scolded, as Connor gave the address to the policeman. "There's just no one there!" She angrily pulled the receiver from his hand.

"Sorry to have wasted your time, constable," Carol said to the unhappy sergeant on the other end of the line. "My husband sleepwalks," she lied, making Connor angry.

*Who the bloody hell is she to suggest that I imagined this?* Connor thought.

As if reading his thoughts, Carol coldly turned on Connor, "Damn you! There's just nobody out…"

The crashing of the door as it burst off its hinges interrupted her, breaking the silence of the still night. It flew past them and smashed loudly into the far wall, showering wood, dust, and glass fragments in all directions.

The creature quickly followed through the broken door frame and into the room. Its hood caught on a large protruding piece of wood, and pulled it back from its head, revealing its grotesque appearance. The grey thin face had no nose, but slanted black eyes that seemed to curl around on each side of its temples, although one eye seemed strangely blank and unfocused. Its head was mainly bald, but sprouted tufts of green like hair that grew out at odd angles and different lengths. Some of the tufts flowed down past its waist, while others ended as small nubs, almost where they began. It slowly opened its shallow lips, showing row upon row of black, pointed shark-like teeth. Carol fainted as something behind the teeth moved like a small, yellow snake.

The giant creature levitated into the centre of the room, hovering about a foot from the floor, arms at its sides. From the phone that Carol had dropped to the floor, a barely audible, distant voice was reprimanding them for wasting police time. Moving its head from side-to-side, the creature pointed a gnarled hand at them.

Carol regained consciousness quickly, but almost swooned again as the creature moved toward her.

"What is it?" she screamed at the cowering Connor, who was desperately trying to crawl away through the empty doorway.

Screams and cries of agony filled the phone's receiver. "What in Gods name are you?" a man's horrified voice whispered hoarsely.

The distinct sound of glass breaking and wood cracking could be heard. Then there were the screams.

"Good God," said Sergeant Hutchison as he listened to the carnage on the other end of the phone line. "Hello," he shouted, "hello…"

It was a short time later when the police car skidded up to the door, and the men quickly exited from it.

"Jesus Christ," muttered Constable Watson, as the small band of policemen entered the house. The scene they were witnessing was something sent straight from hell.

Sergeant Hutchison gently pushed Watson aside, and beheld a sight he hoped he would never see again. Yet, he held his composure as Watson belched, and made quickly for the door. He was unable to reach it in time, and he threw up all over his new uniform. Watson turned to look at the sergeant, before collapsing against the wall.

"What in God's name has happened here?" the sergeant whispered to himself, as he stared at the ravaged body parts that were torn and scattered all over the large room.

Bloody streaks stained the walls and Constable Watson stared at them in terror. Furniture lay broken and discarded all over the room, and the men noticed that all the windows and mirrors were completely shattered.

Revolver in hand, Sergeant Hutchison walked slowly outside and looked around, but the place was deserted.

"Jimmy, pull yourself together and radio for reinforcements," he said, trying to find his strength and regain his authority.

"Yes-sar-re-re in-inforc…"

"Good God, man, give me the bloody radio!" Sergeant Hutchison said. He abruptly snatched the radio from Constable Watson's shaking hands.

Soon the area was teeming with police and forensic people. The sergeant instructed Constable Watson to take the rest of the night off.

"Constable Rice, take this man home, he's unfit for duty. Then hurry back," he ordered, pointing at Jimmy.

"Ok sarge, Right away. C'mon, Jimmy," Rice said to Constable Watson.

Soon the two men were driving away from the old house, and down the wet, winding country roads.

"Who could have done something like this?" Constable Ferris asked Sergeant Hutchison , as he pulled at a small, upturned table.

"I don't know son, but what I heard down the phone line as those people were being slaughtered was something I never wish to hear again."

"Are you alright Jimmy?" Constable Rice asked the still shaking Watson, as he drove along the dark wet country road

"I,-I have never witnessed anything like that before, P-Peter," he stuttered to the older, more experienced policeman.

"Well, you'll get over it. Don't worry, lad."

"It wa…"

"What in heaven's name?" interrupted Constable Rice as he braked hard on the pedals.

The car skidded from left to right before coming to a halt on the wet, deserted road.

Up ahead, right in front of them—it hovered. There above the centre line—about three feet off the ground. Its large silhouette stood out, brilliant in the glistening moonlight. Its dark cape fluttered in the wind.

"Jesus Christ, Peter, what is it?" Constable Watson screamed. "Where's your fucking gun?" he yelled, forgetting that only sergeants were authorised to carry firearms.

"I'm unarmed, Jimmy," Constable Rice whispered.

"Turn the car Peter, turn the car—for Jesus sake turn the car," Constable Watson shouted, his voice rasping.

As Constable Rice pushed and pulled at the gear lever, he ground it into the wrong gear—stalling the car. Jimmy leaned out of his open window, and squinted as he scanned left and right. The road was now empty. He almost fell out of the car as he leaned further out for a better look. "It's gone, Peter!" he declared, as he pulled himself back in. He turned to look at Constable Rice, who was now sitting headless in the driver's seat, door ajar.

The windscreen, steering wheel and dashboard were covered in Constable Rice's blood. Watson froze in terror as he watched Constable Rice's body convulse. One of Rice's hands held fast to the steering wheel and twitched. The wheel turned from side to side, causing the car to shudder and vibrate.

Constable Watson panicked as he groped for the door handle. He noticed that the right sleeve of his tunic was dripping blood, before he felt the pain suddenly shoot up his arm and across his body. He had been cut, and badly. As he pulled the ripped sleeve off his jacket, he saw the deep wound that ran across his arm. Blood was pumping profusely, and furiously from the wound. He clutched the injury with his hand.

Watson had not felt the cut. Not so much as a pinprick, but he knew the injury was life threatening. Then, and without any warning, the car was lifted from the ground, turned over and flung down hard on its roof. There was a deafening bang, and he fell in a heap on the hard ceiling.

The headless body of Constable Rice rolled over Watson's legs, and he kicked hard at his body as he scrambled to get out. After a brief struggle, the car door finally swung open. He slowly stood up, scanned all around, and saw that the wet, moonlit road was once again deserted.

Watson staggered away from the scene clutching at his arm, and prayed. Thoughts of his daughter and grandson were the only things that ran through his mind now.

Watson's only child, Jayne, had always been the apple of his eye. Then when little Ryan came along, and Jayne's boyfriend deserted her, he was left to help her take care of the baby. His wife had walked out on him when Jayne was only two years old, and he had never heard from her again. But he had managed, and now he was happy with just the three of them.

Watson moved faster now, down the empty road, looking at every hedge and tree as he went. He didn't want to die, and leave Jayne and Ryan—but he had witnessed the speed and power of this merciless creature. It spared no-one, and he knew the odds of surviving this night were stacked heavily against him.

Watson felt sick, and felt his stomach heave as he moved on down the dark wet road. He clumsily removed his belt, pulled off the useless pouches, and wrapped it around his bleeding arm. He pulled it tight like a tourniquet. He knew he would bleed to death, if the belt didn't hold.

A sudden movement from the bushes attracted his attention. He was sure it was there, lurking, ready to pounce.

"What the hell is keeping Rice?" Sergeant Hutchison asked.

"I'll contact him now sarge," answered Constable Shields.

"My-my…" the sergeant said, as he surveyed the carnage before him, and shook his head despairingly.

"They're not answering their bloody radio, sarge," Constable Shields announced.

"Jimmy," shouted the sergeant as he rushed for the door.

Hutchison had known Jimmy Watson since they were children, and an almost brotherly like bond had formed between the two men over the years. OK so he had been hard on Jimmy since he had joined the Garda just six months ago, but it was all for the man's own good.

Hutchison couldn't show favouritism, not in front of the others anyway. Now though, he felt fear. Something wasn't right. He knew it, a gut feeling. A feeling he had experienced a hundred times before, and a feeling that seldom let him down.

"Shields, Brannigan, Ferris, follow me," Hutchison ordered, as he ran for the police car, dived in and slammed the door. Then they were speeding off down the narrow country road, siren blaring.

As the big car sped into the corners, no one in the vehicle spoke a word. These events had come upon them so quickly, events of the sort that they had never encountered before. This was policing on a different level, and it was alien to all of them.

*Nothing exciting or dangerous has ever happened down here. Not on this scale,* Sergeant Hutchison thought. Then he thought about Jimmy, and his mind wandered back to when he was a teenage boy.

*He had just stormed from the gates of old Branyan's Orchard. His cardigan was swelling to the neck with apples, and as he ran, some spilled out onto the lane. He must have looked a pretty amusing sight, as the apples bounced from his waistband into the hedges. But he would not stop to pick any up. Not with Branyan's men hot on his tail.*

43

*There had been five of them when they entered the orchard by the rear fence. He had been their leader, with young Jimmy Watson as second in command, the Pierce twins came next, and at the bottom of the chain, came Henry Hollow.*

*His real name was Henry Martin, but because of his very low intelligence, the kids at school had named him, "Henry Hollow." He didn't seem to mind, or even care about the reason why though. All he knew was that he had friends who accepted him, cared for him, and had fun with him. But the boys had really only let Henry tag along because of his enormous size. This, they believed, helped to scare off rival gangs.*

*The day they entered the orchard, Jimmy had pleaded with the other boys not to let Henry go.*

*'He's only going to slow us down and get us caught. Besides, he's got a cold,' Jimmy had proclaimed.*

*But the other boys would hear none of it. Why should they take all the risks, while Henry would get to eat most of the apples? So Henry Hollow went along.*

*The boys had picked their fill, and were about to leave the quiet orchard, when Branyan's granddaughter came into view. She was accompanied by two other girls, whom the boys didn't recognise. Cousins, or friends, perhaps.*

*The boys hid behind the apple trees, and they stood still, barely breathing. Henry's size made it almost impossible for him to hide. Even though he stood behind a very large tree, his huge midriff stuck out over the sides. The boys pointed at each other, and at Henry, knowing they were going to be caught at any second now. But the girls walked passed, without even noticing them.*

*Jimmy had just heaved a sigh of relief, when suddenly, Henry sneezed. Not a small, hold your nose sniffled sneeze, but a loud full blown atishoo, that covered his entire mouth and chin with green snot.*

*They were caught! And as the girls yelled at the top of their voices, the boys put into action their only effective escape plan—they ran!*

*Branyan's men, attracted by the girls yells, quickly ran from the house and gave chase. Soon they caught Henry and then Jimmy, who had doubled back to help him.*

*Branyan and his men beat the two boys badly when they refused to name the other boys involved in the theft of the apples. The boys returned, blackened and bruised, but Jimmy had a tale to tell that would push Henry Hollow back up the chain of command, perhaps to the very highest level.*

*Everyone in the village knew that Branyan was a tyrant and a bully. His cruel streak had a reputation that ran the length and breadth of Ireland. But no one ever thought of standing up to him, because he owned most of the land in the area, and was responsible for employing nearly a quarter of the men living in Cappawhite. Branyan must have thought that Henry would be the weaker of the two boys, and ordered him to be stripped to the waist and dragged out into a clearing. Once there, Henry would be beaten with straps until he talked.*

*As Branyan and his two farm workers started to beat Henry, he jumped up and punched one of them, knocking him down. The man was obviously hurt and lay unmoving on the ground. Jimmy stood astounded, as he watched the second younger man charge at Henry, but he, too, met the same fate. Seeing two of his strongest men fall, Branyan beat a hasty retreat. Henry quickly, although clumsily, followed him, and kicked him on the seat of his pants, sending Branyan sprawling, face down into a small puddle of mud.*

*'Go Henry,' Jimmy shouted, as he picked up Henry's clothes and waved to him. Then the two boys ran from the orchard.*

*The boys tried to re-name Henry, Henry the Bear after this, but the name Hollow had stuck. So he was to be "Henry Hollow" until the day he died. This was when he was killed in a car accident, just five years later. He was only eighteen years of age.*

Constable Watson could hear the siren way off in the distance, coming for him. He would have to go back to the car to get to the radio. He must warn them, stop them somehow. Watson turned and ran back toward the upended car, extremely aware of the presence that he knew was near. He was certain that it was going to kill him—any moment now.

Watson knew that he could not let these men come here to be slaughtered. The effortless and speedy way that this thing killed Constable Rice, was testament to its power. He shuddered, thinking again of the police car with Constable Rice's headless body inside. It was still someway off in the distance. He could see the car, in front, lying silently on its roof. He felt nauseated at the thought of going back inside the car. Yet, he bravely ran on, panting and struggling up the hill.

Breathless and drained of strength, Watson leaned heavily on the bottom of the door, and reached inside for the radio, fumbling and groping in the darkness. There was no time for call signs, no time for procedure. He knew it was Sergeant Hutchison, his friend, driving the police car with the siren blaring, because none of the others at the house were authorised to drive.

"Stay away, sarge, stay away! It's killed Peter, and it will kill us all. Stay away," Watson urged into the microphone.

The policemen in the speeding car stared at one another for a moment, frightened at what they were hearing.

"Maybe we should stay away, sarge," Constable Ferris muttered nervously.

"Stay away my arse," Sergeant Hutchison rasped, as he skilfully manoeuvred the big car into the bends of the road. Jimmy was his best friend, and the sergeant could feel his adrenaline rush as he pushed the car as hard as it would go.

Constable Watson could hear shuffling, like branches shaking violently in the wind. "My God," he whispered to himself as the giant figure came out slowly. Its height towered over the tallest of the bushes.

Struggling for breath, Watson sat down on the wet ground and removed his wallet. He stared at the photo inside and grinned awkwardly. The two smiling, unmoving faces of Jayne and baby Ryan stared back out at him. He kissed the photo for the last time as the giant creature manoeuvred itself above him. Blood ran across his hand like a little stream and forced its way across his wallet, partly covering the photographs, but Jimmy swiped it away with a bloodied hand. Then he gently closed the wallet, placing it behind him.

The rain was heavier now as the police car skidded around the corner, window wipers beating fast. The creature came into view in the powerful beams of the headlights, and Constable Ferris gave a yell.

"Easy, son," said Sergeant Hutchison as he stopped the car about twenty feet away from the other, overturned police vehicle.

"Get bloody back, you fiend!" he shouted frantically, as he exited the car, revolver in hand. But the beast ignored him as it hovered menacingly over Constable Watson.

"Shoot it, sarge," yelled Constable Ferris as he nervously hid behind the sergeant. Hutchison was still fumbling furiously with the gun. "Shoot it, shoot it" he repeated.

Sergeant Hutchison carefully aimed the revolver at the beast. "Get back or I'll fucking shoot you," he warned, matter of factly, with no sign of fear in his voice.

Suddenly the creature spun around and faced the men, and they drew back in sheer terror. Nothing could have prepared them for this. No manual in the world could have advised them about something this evil, and now it was down to basic human survival. The creature moved slowly toward them.

"Shoot the fucking thing! Shoot, sarge!" Brannigan and Shields shouted simultaneously. Constable Ferris, almost breathless from fear, moved behind the police car, opened the trunk and climbed inside.

Suddenly the quiet of the night was interrupted by three shots as the sergeant fired into the beast.

"Good God," he exclaimed, as the beast came on, levitating slowly towards them.

"Shoot it in the head," yelled Shields.

Hutchison took careful aim and blasted another three shots into its head. Small pieces of its leathery skin seemed to blow from its hood, but still, on it came.

The sergeant had no bullets left, but he knew they would be useless anyway. He dropped his arms to his side. The revolver slipped from his sweaty palm, clunking to the hard ground as the creature hovered before him. Hutchison took one last sad look over at his friend Jimmy, who sat with his head in his hands, muttering a quick prayer. Then he closed his eyes.

# CHAPTER 4

Donald O'Shea wandered into the hallway of the Dublin police station, and stopped to ponder for a moment. Briefcase in hand, he stood under the large reprint of the *le Bonheur De Vivre* (The joy of life), that adorned the station wall, and stared solemnly up at it.

Donald was sad that it would be his last week on the job, but conceded that now at last Heather and he could take the time to do the things they had often talked about. It had been a great career for him, with plenty of wonderful memories, although some quite painful. But he had earned a good living from the job, and had saved a nice little nest egg that would keep them both in relative comfort for the rest of their days. Getting to the position of Superintendent was by no means an easy achievement, and he felt proud, but sad, as he slowly sauntered through the large mahogany doors.

Donald's son, Ian, had jokingly taunted him, going on about his retirement, reminding his dad of just how old he really was. Yet, Donald had always kept himself in good shape, and could have passed for a man ten years younger anyway.

As he entered the hallway, Sergeant Gourley approached him.

"Hello, Robin," Donald said. "How are you?"

"Did you hear about the murders, sir?" the sergeant asked.

"Murders? No. What murders?"

"Um… six policemen and two civilians, sir. The report said they were all torn to pieces."

"Here in Dublin?" Donald enquired.

"No, sir. Over in county Tipperary, at a little place called Cappa…"

"White," Donald said loudly, interrupting him, as he dropped his briefcase to the floor. He held the wall for support, his head spinning.

"You alright, sir?" the sergeant asked.

Donald stood silent for a moment before speaking, trying to take in what he had just heard.

"Otis," he whispered to the confused sergeant. "Otis," he repeated.

Donald always had this feeling. No, not a feeling; a firm belief that he would hear about Otis again sometime in his future. It had all just ended too damn suddenly thirty-five years ago.

*What in God's name is happening here,* Donald thought. He had always been one of life's wonderer's. Wondering why he was put on this earth, and wondering where he was going in life? *Maybe this police work was just a front to a greater plan,* he thought. *Maybe God had brought me here for a purpose that I wasn't to know about until the time came. And maybe, just maybe, this is the time.* If God wanted this from him, then so be it. He would walk into the Valley of the Shadow of Death, or anywhere else the Lord had in mind for him. In fact, in a weird way he somehow felt proud that the Lord had chosen him.

Donald thought suddenly of Humphrey Bogart and Bogart's voice filled his head.

*"Why in all the joints in all the world, you hadda walk into mine,"* the voice said.

This wasn't some mad religious belief that had suddenly taken hold of his body, eclipsing all his other feelings, because even as a child—Donald had known about the supernatural.

*The first time it happened to him was when his old Aunt Dorothy lay dying, and the family had been called to her bedside. Donald had not been allowed to go into the actual room, but the old woman had wakened and asked for him.*

*This seemed strange to everyone, because Dorothy had never been very close to Donald. In fact, Dorothy didn't even like children. Yet, she made such a fuss that the family felt compelled to bring the boy to her bedside.*

*"I must speak to Donald alone," she had ordered.*

*After some discussion, the family grudgingly agreed, and to Donald's dismay, filed from the room. Soon Dorothy was left alone with the frightened child.*

*"Come closer, boy," she breathed, in small, panting gasps.*

*Donald shuffled in his seat and pretended to move closer, but in actuality, he hadn't moved more than an inch. His ugly, old aunt repulsed him with her wrinkly, leathery brown skin, large bulging eyes, straw-like hair, and her funny smell.*

*"Take my hand," Dorothy croaked.*

*Donald slowly moved his hand forward, afraid, even though his mother had assured him everything would be alright. He loosely held his aunts cold, stiff hand, and a shiver ran down his spine.*

*"Listen to me child," she whispered, as she looked across the room to make sure no one was listening.*

*Donald felt sure she was going to tell him the biggest secret since the beginning of all time, and he waited in anticipation. She struggled, but somehow managed to lean across to him. Her stale breath wafted into his face, and he grimaced. Donald gulped with fear as her grip on him increased, hurting him.*

*"I have a message for you, my boy. A day is going to come—many years from now. On a day when you think you have just finished your life's calling. When that day comes, and come it will, you will be confronted by a creature from the dark side. In fact, many horrific creatures. Remember, God will be with you—right beside you during those dark hours. And you must be brave," Aunt Dorothy coughed loudly, and a large piece of flem forced its way from her wrinkled lips and landed on his sleeve.*

*Donald wrenched his hand free, and cried. He ran out from the room, and his aunt shouted after him, "He will be with you boy. The Lord God will be with you."*

*The family gathered around the frightened child and comforted him.*

*"I told you not to leave Donald alone with her," someone exclaimed.*

*A white mist suddenly darted across the ceiling, and Donald seemed to be the only one to notice it. He pointed up at the ceiling, afraid, and sobbing.*

*"What the hell is wrong with that boy?" someone asked.*

*"She's dead," a voice boomed out from Dorothy's room.*

*"Are you alright, Donald?" His uncle asked.*

Then the voice changed suddenly, dragging Donald back to the present.

"Are you alright, sir, are you alright?" Sergeant Gourley asked him as he gently prodded Donald's chest with his finger.

Donald shook his head groggily, and snapped out from his dream state.

"Sorry, um, Sergeant Gourley, and yes, I'm alright. Thank you," he answered.

Miles away on a country road, just outside of Cappawhite, a car phone rang and a young constable answered. After a pause, he crossed the road to where a bunch of senior policemen were busy trying to take stock of events from the night before.

"Phone call for you, sarge," he said to Sergeant McCann, who was busy trying to brief the inspectors as to what was going on. The sergeant slumped into the police car, and picked up the car phone.

"Hello, Sergeant McCann speaking."

"Hello Blair, its Donald O'Shea here. I just heard the news. So it's Otis? He's returned then."

"Hello, Donald. I mean, Sir, and yes, I believe so. I'm at the scene now. Bloody body parts were strewn everywhere when we got here. Six policemen dead at the scene, and two police cars totally wrecked. Sergeant Hutchison was one of the men," he added sadly.

Donald had known Sergeant Hutchison as a constable and had recommended him for the sergeant's post all those years ago. Now he thought of these poor policemen's families, and how someone was going to have to break the news to them. God alone knew how many times he'd had to tell the loved ones that someone dear to them had died or been killed. Not a pleasant duty. Even for an officer as experienced such as he was. The way these men had been killed though, was a whole new level of brutality.

*What a terrible bloody waste of life,* Donald thought. "Sarah, she must have died then?" he stated suddenly.

"That could be. We could do with your help over here, Donald. Um, sorry, Sir," Sergeant McCann corrected himself again. "In any event, you and I are the only ones left who have actually witnessed this creature."

"I will be with you as soon as I can--as soon as I can make some arrangements," Donald assured him.

# CHAPTER 5

Back in LA, Dan Winters entered his office, and stared down at the pink envelope that sat just where he had left it. It was a full half-hour before he had finished reading the old woman's account of the happenings in Cappawhite. He was stunned. This was not the writings of a deranged mind, but a meticulous, well put together account of someone who seemed to know what they were talking about. It read like a horror novel. Yet, far fetched as the story seemed to him, he was going to look into it.

Dan started by recalling up the events of the slaying of Miguel Santos in Sarah's apartment, and the autopsy report. Santos's head had been ripped from his body by some unknown force. The force was so strong that it had caused fractures around the skull and left shoulder. The pancreas had been in a fairly advanced state of cancer, and in the pathologist's opinion, incurable. Santos would have been lucky to have survived another four months of life anyway, had he not been killed. The coroner believed it was a gangland slaying, but could offer no suggestion as to the implements they used to tear the man's head off. However, the force needed would have had to have been exceedingly powerful. The coroner also stated that Santos had been alive when his head was ripped off. Blood spatter evidence, the arterial spray, just about streaked on every wall of the room, seemed to support that claim.

Dan had always thought it was implausible that Sarah had slept through that sort of commotion. *How could a woman sleep through a man having his head ripped off in her apartment?* he thought. But now as he read Sarah's letter, Dan found himself almost believing the words before him. Gradually, Sarah opened up more and more, and told her story...

At the end of her letter, Sarah revealed that Santos was threatening to rape her when Otis appeared. And that this thing, which once was Otis, had effortlessly torn the man's head off... Sarah's life and dignity had been saved. Even if it was in the most sickening way imaginable.

Dan had read Sarah's account of Otis turning into this creature with great scepticism, Yet, he could not get away from the fact that the old woman's written account somehow tied in with the evidence from the crime scene.

*This is crazy*, Dan thought as he stared at the old woman's letter. Then he reached over to the intercom and buzzed the outer office. "Bennett, get your butt in here," he ordered.

It was a full two minutes before Bennett sheepishly entered Dan's office.

"Yeah?" Bennett asked.

"Go get me anything you can on a small town named "Cappawhite" in Ireland. Anything from late 1967," Dan ordered.

"What sort of things?" enquired Bennett, sounding disinterested, as he fidgeted with his watch strap, annoyingly opening and closing it.

"Murders, supernatural stuff, any goddamn thing," Dan answered, raising his voice. "Just freakin' do it!" He waved his arms like an out of synch choirmaster trying to conduct Bennett out of his office. Dan slammed the door behind the kid, and mumbled to himself.

Outside the door, Bennett held his middle finger up to the office door in a gesture of defiance. "Asshole," he whispered.

Bennett didn't like Dan. He was sick and tired being talked down to all the time. If it wasn't for his damn mother, and how she would yell at him—he would have left this sorry-assed job months ago. He didn't even want to be a reporter. He would have been fine working down at Sal's Pizza with all his other buddies. There was a place, at least, where he would be appreciated. And if the tips his buddies had bragged about were anything to go by, then he would be made. But his mother would have none of it, so it looked like he would be stuck here for some time.

Then there was the issue of Dan Winter's wife, Beatrice. It had become a kind of office joke because of the way she treated Dan. She would constantly phone him to complain about every stupid little thing she could think off. If they ran into any of the other office staff, when they were out in town, Beatrice would snub them, and act as if they weren't even there. Instead of standing up to the crazy bitch, Dan would come into work and brood over his sad, sorry life. Then he would take it out on anyone stupid enough to cross him in any way.

Suddenly the phone in Dan's office rang. When he answered it, he was surprised to hear Beatrice on the other end of the line.

"Mother just fell at the nursing home. They think she's broken her leg," she sobbed.

"Well, I'll come by and get you and…"

"No," Beatrice interrupted. "I rang Philip, and he's going to take me. You stay away."

"Phil, your brother is going to take you..?" Dan asked, puzzled, as Beatrice slammed the phone down and cut him off in mid sentence.

*Why Beatrice hadn't seen Phil in about five years, and neither had her mother. What the hell is he doing crawling back onto the scene now?* Dan thought. *Unless, it has something to do with the old woman's will. Maybe that drugged-up sonofabitch thinks she hasn't long to go. Maybe like a hyena, he thinks he can scavenge some of the remains of the old woman's belongings. Then slink off into the night, and back to the rat hole that he crawled outta.*

Sometime later, the door to Dan's office burst open and an excited Bennett came charging in. "Mr Winters," he called and waved a sheet of freshly printed paper like a flag. "I was checking out Cappawhite for you, when a big news bulletin appeared. It's all over the news over there."

"What is? What news? Over where?" Dan asked.

"Five or six cops and a couple of civilians were killed in Cappawhite last night. The Irish army has been mobilised, and all police leave cancelled."

"You shitting me, Bennett?"

"No. Honest, Mr Winters, go check it out for yourself."

"Have they arrested anyone yet?" Dan sat upright in his chair, and squinted one eye.

"According to this report, no, but they are combing the surrounding countryside, looking for whoever was responsible."

"Do they say how these people died?" Dan asked.

"No, but I checked with Burkett, in our London office. He heard that the men's deaths were horrendous, but he could get no details. He also reckons there's some sort of cover up going down over there."

"Well done, kid," Dan said. Impulsively, he patted Bennett on his head and ran from the office with Sarah's envelope tightly squeezed in his hand. "Carry on and find out what you can about the late 1960's in Cappawhite," Dan shouted back as an afterthought.

"I've already done that," answered Bennett.

Dan stopped in his tracks as Bennett talked on.

"Something happened in the village during November 1967. A priest was shot dead, and a few people were killed. And get this, one of the victims was an Afro-American ex cop by the name of 'Otis Tweedy.' They never did find his body. The whole village was evacuated afterward. Some people reported that a demon was responsible, but the Irish government denied this. Their report said it was a chemical spillage which caused everyone in the village to have a mass hallucination."

Dan put his hand on the boys shoulder, and Bennett flushed slightly with embarrassment. "Well done boy, well done," he repeated.

Bennett left the office smiling and proudly sauntered toward the coke machine. *Maybe Dan isn't such a bad guy after all,* he thought.

# CHAPTER 6

Back in Ireland, Donald O'Shea sat with his head in his hands and pondered. As a young Constable he had witnessed one of these abominations, and the power it possessed. This beast that Otis had now become however was obviously much more violent and dangerous than anything they had witnessed before though. It was also much bigger and stronger, he believed.

*Why now?* He wondered, after all these years. *It could only be that Sarah, who would have been an old woman by now, must have died. He knew as they all did, that Sarah had moved back to America soon after Otis had been killed, and they all knew that this demon, or whatever it was had surely gone after her. Just as Emily had done with Mrs Doyle. They had said very little at the time, preferring to keep the matter as low a profile as was possible. But now, God help them, their silence had come back to haunt them,* he thought.

Donald had thought about Sarah quite often over the years, and the guilt he had felt for not following up with her had burdened him ever since. Now this feeling of guilt had trebled. But what could he have done anyway. The power of this Creature was awesome. Donald had witnessed it first hand, and even now the thought of it frightened him. But he had promised Sergeant McCann that he would return to Cappawhite to try and help them out, and by God, dangerous as it was, this is what he intended to do. All of the other people who witnessed this creature had long since died. Most of them from natural cause's in their sleep. One of these deaths though, wasn't so natural, and Donald just didn't like to think about it. But it had ended badly for Constable Pearson. He had been having horrific dreams. Dreams that were so bad they had driven the mild mannered cop to madness. Constable Pearson had been sent to six different psychiatrists over the last two years of his life. Ending his last visit with the most expensive doctor in Harley Street. But they had all asked the same questions, blaming it on some sort of childhood trauma that his family had kept secret. He had even been given electric shock therapy over the last weeks as he continued to withdraw into his mind, and his condition worsened. But the doctors had refused to even contemplate the notion of a Demon, so Donald had stepped in, informing the doctors that he too had witnessed this creature. But when he received no reply, he believed the doctors had thought him also to be mad.

Then he later heard that Constable Pearson had died screaming in the night, and Donald felt sick to the pit of his stomach. But from now on, if asked, Donald would no longer try to hide what he had seen. Because as sure as there was a cloud in the sky, he had seen it, and that was all that mattered. *But all of the men who had witnessed the beast had been left scars of sorts that would never leave them,* he thought.

Dan Winters didn't like Alf Reynolds, but there was a story here and he needed his green for go on it. Reynolds had been his boss for as far back as Dan cared to remember, and in all that time Dan had never seen him smile. Reynolds ran the paper with an iron fist, and whoa betides anyone who crossed him. The staff had instructions to address him as Mr Reynolds or sir, which didn't make the working atmosphere very pleasant, and sometimes Dan wondered how he had stuck the job out for so long. Dan hated the guy! From his high pitched squeaky voice to his cheap ten dollar plastic shoes.

He also hated the way he sometimes had to lick Reynolds fat ass when he needed a story passed, but this was the way it was, and he supposed always would be.

But there was one thing he had to admit about the man. Reynolds was once the best damn reporter in the state. And this wasn't just Dan's opinion. Why the four walls of Reynolds office were testament to this. Awards galore hung from ceiling to floor, adorning every wall, with barely room for a fly to land between the gaps of the frames. Dan always felt humbled when he entered his own office with the two oversized frames that hung five feet apart, strategically placed so that anyone entering his office would automatically zoom in on the certificates.

But Reynolds had at one time thought Dan to be his best and had told him so. That was three years ago though, and he had never praised him again.

As Dan entered his office, Reynolds spoke first. "Get yourself down to the cemetery Winters, and see what you can find out about the old woman."

"Old woman?" Dan asked, puzzled.

"Yeah, goddamn grave robbers snuck in there in the middle of the night two nights ago and stole an old woman's body. They murdered the gravedigger. Beheaded the poor bastard. But the old woman's body was missing. Until now that is! Found the corpse last night, lying in a field, ten miles away. Coffin was wrecked, headstones all busted up all over the goddamn place, and extensive damage done to the grave itself."

"Who was she?" Dan asked

"Some old gal by the name of Sarah Tweedy," Reynolds answered.

Dan staggered back and fell down into the seat. He felt numb. His file slipped from his hand and dropped to the floor without him even noticing. "You alright there Winters?" Reynolds asked loudly, "you need an ambulance or something?"

After a moment Dan pulled himself together and picked the file up from the floor which he handed to Reynolds. "Check the name out, Mr Reynolds," he said anxiously.

"Why it-it says here, Sarah Tweedy?" Reynolds answered, surprised.

"Sure does Alf," Dan answered, which brought him a stern side glance.

Dan explained about Sarah's letter and about the killings back in Ireland that could be linked to her. "Well, looks like we got the makings of a fine story here, I can damn taste it. Now I want you to go over there and check it out?" Reynolds ordered.

"Go over where?" Dan asked, puzzled.

"Why I'm talking about Ireland, damn it Winters, where do you goddamn think?" Reynolds spat.

"No, I can't Mr Reynolds, I can't leave Beatrice alone, she's unwell," Dan said firmly.

"Did you just say no to me? Now you listen to me, and you listen good Winters," he raged. "You just happen to be working for the biggest newspaper in the state. It's in your damn contract to visit any safe country where you're told to go. If you wanna keep your ass in the job then you're just going to have to make other arrangements for your wife. Send that office boy in here, um, Benteen…"

"Bennett, it's Bennett," Dan said, interrupting.

"Yeah, whatever, send him in. I'll need him to make the necessary arrangements for you. I want you over there within the next two days."

Dan left Reynolds office angry and confused at his boss's uncompassionate attitude, and wondered how he was going to tell Beatrice. *God only knows how she will react to being left alone,* he thought. *Why she would be liable to do anything.* But he could do nothing about it. Without his job, the situation at home would only grow worse.

*Try telling that to Beatrice though,* he thought. He would just have to be firm. No matter. He was going and that was the end of the story.

He felt however, that a couple of days in Ireland would see him get to the bottom of the murders, and he would return before Beatrice had time to even realise he had gone. Besides, he had always wanted to visit Ireland and part of him, he felt, was eager to go anyway. But his main concern was Beatrice, although he could never understand why he continued to let her treat him the way she did. It had been a sort of a gradual process, he felt. And just like growing old, he hadn't really noticed it as the years went past. But now it was bad. As bad as it could get! He had gone alone to see a councillor, when Beatrice refused point blank to accompany him, or even talk to him about it. But the female councillor seemed more concerned for his wife than him, and even insinuated that his job at the paper was to blame. But Dan didn't know any other type of work. And besides, most jobs nowadays meant long hours away from home anyway.

Then he thought about Lynn again.

*Beatrice and Lynn had been like chalk and cheese regarding their different personalities. Lynn was so easy going and happy go lucky, that he could honestly never remember even having an argument with her. They had been so happy together then, during those six months of marriage, although they had been dating for almost three years before their marriage. Beatrice on the other hand was cold and aloof, and was always demanding that things go her way or not at all. But when Dan first met her he wasn't even thinking about getting into another relationship.*

*Even though it had been a lonely two years since Lynn and the baby were killed.*

*It was his buddies, Des and Walter who persuaded him to go out with the beautiful model. Always going on at him about what he was missing, and always talking about how great their own damn marriages were.*

*Dan was always a practical guy though, and deep down he knew they were right. This is what Lynn would have wanted for him too, he felt. To be happy again, and get along with his humdrum life.*

*When their relationship had first started though, Beatrice had seemed interesting and kind, and everyone thought of how great a couple they made. But from the very outset, Dan had some doubts. When he mentioned some of these doubts to his friends though, they accused him of being petty. Like the time he gave his young next door neighbour a lift home from work, when her car was in being repaired, and the girl had given him a peck on the cheek. Beatrice had been coming to his home and was just crossing the road at the time and had seen them, but had not mentioned it to Dan. Then, next day at work when he bumped into his young colleague and neighbour, she ignored him. But Dan went ahead and offered her another lift home anyway. The girl clearly was embarrassed and made an excuse to him. Making him feel as though he were some sort of damn pervert who had tried it on with her. But then as Dan was walking angrily away, she called him back. The young girl seemed to have read his body language though.*

'It's nothing that you have done Mr Winters, it's just that I received this,' she said, as she handed Dan a small unsigned note. Dan slowly took the note from her hand and whispered the words. 'Stay away from Dan Winters, or you will not see Christmas you fucking guttersnipe. Just back off!' Then it was Dan's turn to feel embarrassed, because he knew who had sent it, and he mumbled an apology and left. Later that night when he called for Beatrice, he said one word. 'Why?'

'What do you mean, why?'

'My next door neighbour was told to stay away from me, even though I only gave her a lift home from work. And now that I think of it, you must have seen me get out of my car with her,' he accused.

'I'm not following you. Do you think I'm following you?' Beatrice had answered, angrily. Dan showed her the note that he had taken from the girl without her even noticing. But Beatrice vehemently denied any wrong-doing, and offered to go with him and see the girl. She was so convincing that Dan let the matter drop and said no more about it. Then, and almost a year later, Beatrice had gotten into an argument with another girl on the way out from the dance hall. 'If you want to live to see fucking Christmas you guttersnipe, then just back off,' Beatrice had said, and Dan had remembered the note. What Beatrice had said was almost word for word with the note, and now Dan was convinced she had sent it. But Des and Walter had made him see things differently. 'You showed Beatrice the *note at the time, I take it? Walter asked.*

*'Why yes, I did,' Dan admitted.*

*'Well there you are then. Beatrice called it up from memory,' Walter said, with a smirk, as Des nodded in agreement.*

*Dan had to sort of agree with his friends that this may well be the case, but the doubt stayed in his mind.*

*But there were other things as well though. Silly Little things that meant nothing on their own, but tied together made a much bigger picture.*

*Then there was her secret nature. Sometimes when Dan would ask her where she had been, she simply told him to respect her privacy. And although Dan was not the jealous type, he sometimes wondered if there was anything going on with her.*

*Logic told him that beautiful looking girls like Beatrice did not go through life without guy's trying to hit on them, although Beatrice always insisted that this never happened to her.*

*But this was something he didn't stop to dwell on. Anyway, he was much too busy at the paper. Besides this, Dan reckoned that if he tried to order Beatrice about in any way, she would be outta there quicker than he could whistle Dixie.*

*Because as far as Beatrice went, he soon learnt. It was her way or the highway.*

*So before Dan knew it he was in a full blown relationship, and in even less time, he was married.*

*But even the wedding was over the top, he felt. Costing thousands of dollars more than most other average weddings. With the white horses, and open coach. And the embarrassing over the top tuxedo's, which Beatrice insisted they wore.*

*Then at the wedding, her father made a speech that was sickening in the extreme. As her drunken brother Phil staggered back into the room from the bar and knocked over a table. Threatening anyone with violence that dared come near him. Even though the people were only trying to help him. Then her mother screamed and hollered that she was losing her beautiful daughter, and no-one could consol her. All the while though, Dan's family sat dignified throughout.*

*Dan could never remember having a shittier day and he wondered then about just what he was getting himself into with this crazy mixed up family.*

They had started off by living at the house he shared with Lynn. But this would cause problems early in their marriage, with Beatrice constantly casting up about her. Then Beatrice claimed she had seen Lynn's ghost, and refused to stay one more day in the house. Dan had no choice but to quickly sell up and move out of the home he had loved. A place he was happy in with his wonderful memories.

The move had only been five blocks away, but it was two blocks from her mother's home. This Dan believed had been the reason for Beatrice wanting to move all along, and he felt bad that she would do this to Lynn's memory for an excuse to sell. Referring to the woman to whom Dan still loved as a ghost. The drain on his finances during the move would also cause extra strain on their marriage.

Beatrice's mother had never liked Dan, and wasn't afraid to show her feelings about it. Why Dan could have had his damn ass studded with diamonds and this woman would have still disliked him. Why the woman didn't even seem to like her own husband, or at times her own self for that matter.

But he knew that it wasn't a personal thing. No man. Well, no man on the face of this planet anyway, would have been any good for her damned spoilt daughter.

Now he was within walking distance from her mother's house. And now he knew that he would be seeing an awful lot more of her, and he cringed at the thought.

# CHAPTER 7

Donald O'Shea drove out of Dublin and turned onto the main N-7 road to Limerick, and Cappawhite. The journey would take about three hours, more or less, and he wanted to get there before dark. The scent of the open countryside wafted in through the car window, and he took a deep breath. He had told his wife and son that he would be away for a few days on police business, but he failed to mention the true reason behind it. He just didn't wish to worry them.

Donald was unaware, that back home, Heather was also hiding something just as worrying from him. She had visited the surgeon by appointment the previous day, and he had confirmed her worst fears. The cramps she had been getting down the side of her body had now been fully diagnosed. She had a tumour in her lungs.

The word "inoperable" rang in Heather's ears, and she didn't even remember leaving the hospital to go home. She wasn't even sure how long the doctor had given her—a year, perhaps, with chemo. Heather didn't know how she was going to break the news to her loving husband and son, but tell them she must. It could wait though, at least until after Donald's retirement party. She had arranged it to be a surprise, and enlisted the help of his colleagues. Heather collapsed into a chair, and cried herself to sleep.

As he drove along the wet winding road, Donald's thoughts went back to Cappawhite, all those many years ago when he was a young man, especially to old Mick, who had lived in the old battered caravan. His mother had loaned the caravan to him, and old Mick had stayed in it for almost the entire ten years before he died. He remembered talking to old Mick there one day, about three years after the killings.

Mick had informed Donald that he had went to visit his mad sister, Bridget, at the Richmond Lunatic Asylum in Dublin. It hadn't been a pleasant visit, and one he would never dare repeat.

Donald recalled Mick's words to him:

> *'I had thought about Bridget. And I had accepted the fact that what she did wasn't entirely her fault. The psychiatrists had judged her to be insane, and that is just what she was. As far as I was concerned, God is the only one who can judge her on this. So I had made my mind up that I should like to pay her a visit.*
>
> *It had been so many long years since I last set eyes on her that I was very nervous and feared*

*how I would be accepted by her. When I arrived at the place, I was awed by its professionalism. Stern nurses in starched uniforms mulled about all over the place. The smell of bleach was somewhat overpowering, and when two male orderlies rushed passed me with what looked like a straight jacket in their arms. It was then I realized just what sort of hell hole I was in. The head warden, a Dr Rickman, greeted me with some consternation. I felt somewhat embarrassed by the fact that I hadn't been to visit Bridget before.*

*I must admit that I lost my head for a moment when Dr Rickman broached that very subject. When he informed me that Bridget had nothing of any value locked away under their care—I blew my top. I informed him that I wasn't interested in any of Bridget's possessions. I also told him that Bridget was responsible for the deaths of two of my sisters. In fact, she was almost responsible for my near death, and in a roundabout way, certainly responsible for my wife, Mary's, death.*

*Then I informed the great doctor that I wasn't one of his bloody inmates that he could do anything he damned well pleased with, and would like to be treated with some respect. I think, in the end, his face was redder than mine, and he left the room without so much as a grunt.*

*Of course, if I had told him that I had once seen a real live demon with my own two eyes— he would have probably certified me there and then, and forced me into a straight jacket.*

Finally, I was given the go ahead to visit Bridget, and I took a deep breath when they came to get me. As we moved along the corridor, I was accompanied by three female orderlies. Now all of whom were very big strapping girls, but they all seemed frightened somehow.

When I entered Bridget's small padded cell, the sight shocked me to my core. The pathetic, old figure that once used to be the young, beautiful, energetic sister I knew, sat unmoving on the small bed, staring at the floor. Her skin, or what was left of it, was ashen grey. She was a frail skeleton, and probably weighed no more than four or five stones.

'Hello Bridget,' I called to her, but there wasn't even as much as a blink from her in recognition. I sat beside her for about half-an-hour, talking to her, but I knew then that she was too far gone to know anyone. I told her I forgave her for what she had done, even though that was mostly a lie.

Then just as I got up to leave, I took one last look at her. As I did, I was stunned to see that Bridget was staring right at me. Wide-eyed, her mouth opened and drooling, her green and brown rotting teeth were a horror to behold. Then suddenly she raised her head high, her eyes wide and glaring. Her sunken cheeks, looked almost transparent, and quivered.

'It waits,' Bridget said, in a deep growl. Then, she fell back down onto the bed, as if she was asleep.

Even the orderlies, who had never heard her speak before in all those years, seemed afraid *at this. They all backed off, out into the corridor. I tell you, Donald, I left that place as fast as my legs would bloody take me.*

*Three months later, I was informed that Bridget had died peacefully in her sleep. At least there was mercy for her in the end.'*

This was how old Mick finished the story about his visit to Bridget. And Donald didn't believe that the visit had done the old man any good. Old Mick had tried to cut down on his drinking after this. He believed firmly that if there were demons like the one he had seen Otis fight, then it was only natural to assume that there must be another side. The other side had to be God's.

And, even though he continued to drink, Old Mick prayed every day to the Lord. The Lord that he now believed was as real as the creature he had seen with his own two eyes. His nightmares stopped after this, and a sort of quiet peaceful calm came over him.

Then old Mick had paired off with old Elspeth McGill. Old, drunk, and dancing Elspeth. Soon they were living together in Mick's caravan. Although they were both old, and fond of the drink, a passionate bond formed between them.

Everyone in the town knew just how much they were in love with each other, and it always amazed people to see how courteous old Mick was toward her. Mick knew that Elspeth had as many troubles in her past life as he had. Once a school teacher, she was also a dancer, and had taught all the children at the school to dance. Elspeth, Mick remembered, had been a very beautiful woman then, almost as beautiful as his Mary. In fact, they were really the best looking two girls in the village at that time--apart from Mick's sister, Brenda, Mick knew Brenda was beautiful, but being his sister, he didn't enter her into the equation.

Elspeth explained to Mick that her husband had beaten her very badly at the school. Somehow he had found out that she was having an affair with the headmaster. Elspeth had been hurt very badly by her husband, and had suffered a permanent injury to her head, which caused her to have frequent migraines for years to come. Her husband was jailed for six months after assaulting her, and the three policemen who had come to her rescue.

Her husband was released from prison, after serving only three months. When Elspeth was informed, she panicked, but he would never return to Cappawhite. Elspeth never set eyes on him again, and in her shame over the whole incident, she never returned to the school. Her husbands' belittling and constant abuse had driven her into the arms of another man in the first place. The man had been a religious fanatic, who made her every breathing moment a living hell. He had beaten the defenceless woman at every opportunity. It wasn't that Elspeth had felt any love for Mr Blane, the headmaster, but his friendliness and kindness, and the attention he showed toward her, were things she craved. It was out of need for sheer human kindness that she got involved with the older, married family man.

After Elspeth's husband attacked her at the school, Mr Blane distanced himself from her. The broken woman then hit the bottle after this, spending her life as a near recluse. Then she met old Mick, and it was as though her world had been turned upside down. Even though they were both old, when she looked into old Mick's leathery face, she could only see the handsome man that Mick used to be.

The pair spent many happy years together, before Elspeth died in her sleep. Mick was just as devastated by her passing as he had been when Mary died. He prayed for the Lord to take him also. He would get his wish, but he would have to wait another three lonely years before his prayers were answered.

When Mick took ill, and knew the end was looming, he sent for Donald just before he died. He asked the friendly policeman to look after the precious photographs of his sisters. He wished to have Mary and Elspeth's photograph's buried with him. Donald complied and made sure that the two photos were in his coffin. The rest of the photos were safely tucked away in a drawer in Donald's home, and he prayed that somehow, somewhere, at last they would all be together again.

Someone else would be brought down to earth after old Mick's death. Someone who had never spared a moment's thought for the old man, and continued to despise him, even after his death.

James Flanagan's wife, Rose, had named the baby "Francis," in memory of the child's father, Frank Quinn, the priest. But she had struggled to bring up the girl. An unknown benefactor had been sending her twenty punts religiously every week to help with the child, and this was enough to at least keep some food on the table, and also helped them immensely over the years.

For some reason though, Rose had always believed that the church was responsible for this welcomed gift. Yet, when old Mick died, the money stopped—just when Francis had turned nine years old. Rose approached the church to find out why they had stopped sending her the money, but they informed her that they knew nothing about it. When she went to enquire at the post office though, she learned the truth.

Rose found to her horror that it was the one man she had hated all those years. Old Mick had helped her when others had turned their backs. Old Mick! When Rose learnt of this, she cried, and asked God to forgive her for feeling the way she did about him. She had never given the kind old man a chance. Old Mick had told no one about this secret of his, not even Elspeth.

*Donald had asked for the move from Cappawhite to Dublin on the grounds that he could no longer function properly in the job, after what had happened in the town. The Garda were very obliging to him. His transfer to Dublin was so quick that it had even surprised him. Donald could never feel confident again, working in Cappawhite, patrolling the dark country roads alone.*

*In any event, if he had stayed in Cappawhite, he never would have met Heather. So he was thankful that things had worked out so well for him. Some of his new colleagues had ribbed him at first when he arrived at his new post, as Station sergeant, in Dublin. But after getting to know* him, and his honest ways, most of the men decided to avoid the rumours they had heard about the supernatural happenings in Cappawhite, which frightened and confused some of them.

Donald finally got fed up listening to gossip and speculation of what had happened at Cappawhite—about ghosts, ghouls, spectres, and banshees. He had decided to end them all in one fell swoop, and take a positive action. He gathered all the constables and sergeants together, and bade them to sit down in one of the large briefing rooms.

"I am going to tell you all something," he had said. "This is the true story of the events of Cappawhite. I am going to tell it once and only once, and I will never repeat it again. It is not something I even like to think about nowadays. But I want these rumours and all the talk stopped once and for all. All I can tell you people here today is that I have witnessed, first hand, the abomination that came to our quiet village... If any of you disbelieve me, or don't want to listen, please leave the room now."

Everyone sat rigid in their seat, anxious to hear this honest and respected sergeant's account of the things he had seen.

Donald had told them that first off, this creature was not a Banshee, and about how a very brave Afro American ex-cop named "Otis Tweedy" had journeyed back to America on his own personal quest to find out just what the thing was.

'I am not trying to frighten any of you,' Donald had said. 'But we believe that this creature was only the tip of the iceberg, and that many more *of them exist. I watched as it killed the brave Otis. He did us a huge favour to rid us of it, and my only prayer now, is that it never returns.'*

*When Donald had finished, the men filed from the room in silence. Some of them were visibly shaken by the well-told story. It was clear to all that this wasn't the ramblings of some attention seeker, but a man who was unburdening his soul for all to hear. When he had finished telling it, he had felt a great weight lift from his shoulders.*

Donald had never mentioned the subject again, and buried it away in his subconscious. Now though, it was back, and the memory of his last encounter with it shadowed his every thought.

Another frightening event was to happen to Donald, an event that would again bring Cappawhite to the forefront of his mind.

When Donald had been at Dublin's main station for about a year, he had read something in an aged occurrence book, written by an old sergeant, Brian Devlin, from Cappawhite. Devlin had written a report about a supernatural experience he had dealt with in Cappawhite, shortly after the turn of the century. Although Cappawhite was not in Dublin's jurisdiction, he had written it because it related to a few sketchy events that were also happening in Dublin at the same time.

*1910:*

*This report is from Thomas Fahey, a God fearing, non-drinking man, who before this event would never have believed in such foolish things as he was about to relate.*

*When Thomas Fahey was cycling on his bicycle one night, just as darkness crept in, and he was freewheeling downhill on his approach to Ironmills Bridge, just outside of Cappawhite. A black mass suddenly came from out of nowhere, and landed on the handlebars of his bicycle. Although on a downhill run, the bicycle slowed to almost a stop, even though Fahey began peddling with all his might. He was terrified of the apparition in front of him. The black mass made no sound and no movement, but Fahey knew it was as real as the bicycle he was sitting upon.*

*After what seemed an eternity, and as Fahey neared the bridge, the black mass flew off the handlebars, and quickly disappeared up one of the lanes. And a relieved, but shocked Thomas Fahey, peddled for all he was worth into the safety of the village.*

There were two words written on the side of the page in this report. Two words that someone had written a long time ago, and two words that would have Donald staring at the page for some time:

Bean Sidhe!-(The Banshee!)

These words had frightened Donald when he read them, and at the time, he swore he would only visit Cappawhite and his mother during the daylight hours. As the years passed though, and with no further sightings of anything, Donald's confidence grew. Sometimes he would bring Heather and their son with him for a holiday at his mother's house. As far as he was concerned, the beast had gone and the rest of them could now live their lives in peace.

Yet, Donald would still decline to go walking along the country lanes during the dark hours. Visiting with his mother was one thing, tempting fate was another!

# CHAPTER 8

Ken Tully had loved fishing since he was a little boy, and now, it was his obsession. Madge had finally given up moaning to him about it, and had one day simply packed her clothes and left. Now he could do as he damn well pleased, any time he damn well liked—except now, he didn't want to.

"Tully" as he preferred to be called and how everyone knew him, hadn't realised he had loved Madge as much as he did—until she was gone. Even his job as gamekeeper was being affected, as he began taking more and more time away from work. Now, after eight weeks, he was still a broken man. While in a blind drunken rage, he had snapped all his fishing rods in two, and thrown away his flies, spinners, floats and hooks, along with three whole boxes of fishing bibs and bobs into the river.

It wasn't that Tully was a drinking man, why before Madge left he had hardly touched the stuff. But now, he felt like one of life's losers, and the bottle helped him ease the pain. Tully wanted Madge back. Wanted her back more than life itself, and if that meant giving up the other things he loved most, well then, that's just what he was going to do.

Madge had other plans though. She had waited at home alone almost every night, and had spent many lonely weekends for seemingly countless years while Tully indulged in his passion. Now she wanted something more for herself, and she was going to get it.

Tully waited outside the bingo hall and felt embarrassed as he hid the flowers behind his back. He knew Madge would be coming through the door any minute now, because he knew her obsession with Bingo was as bad as his once was with fishing. Madge and her friend, Erin, had never missed their weekly bingo games in fifteen years, even though she had only won a few times.

When the doors burst open, a stream of women came flooding out, adjusting their coat collars and umbrellas as they stepped into the cold wet night. Tully craned his neck and quickly scanned the faces, looking for her. Then he saw Erin, alone, and his heart sank. He kept the flowers behind his back, but lowered them down, out of sight.

"Where is she?" he snapped at Erin as she walked briskly passed, without noticing him.

Erin didn't want to get involved in their trouble. This was a man and wife thing and none of her business, but Tully had never done her any harm, and she had always liked him. She felt that Madge had overreacted to the man's hobby, and only used it for an excuse to leave him. Madge hadn't even told Erin of her decision, and she had been as much left in the dark as Tully had been when she deserted him.

Erin knew where Madge was staying though, because she had heard old Mrs Rafferty talk about it some weeks ago. She also knew that if old Mrs Rafferty said it, then it was almost sure to be true.

"I don't know where Madge is, Tully," Erin lied.

Then as she turned to walk on, she paused to look back and saw Tully sobbing into a bunch of flowers. She hadn't noticed the flowers, and something about the way he leaned hopelessly into the wall for support, made her feel sad for him. Erin shook her head and compassionately walked back to the distraught man and gently took his arm.

"Are you going to be alright Tully?"

"I love Madge," he groaned. "I need her back. Please help me, Erin.

"She's in Cappawhite," Erin said softly, "staying at The Ross Inn. But if you're thinking of going there, you should just forget about it. All the major roads are blocked, on account of those policemen that got murdered, and the Irish army is on the lookout, searching for the killers."

Impulsively, Erin kissed Tully gently on the cheek, squeezed his arm, and disappeared around the corner.

Tully didn't notice there was someone else missing from the crowd, someone who hadn't walked past him that night. And someone who had other things on their mind right now. Someone who would never return to Tipperary town. Gary Storey had been calling Bingo at the hall for at least ten years, and had just as many affairs tucked below his belt. Each of them petering out almost as quickly as they had began.

This affair was different though. When Gary wooed this beautiful woman he really had called full house. Now at last, he had someone he really wanted to be with. He had felt no guilt when he had lured the vulnerable woman away from her husband. Just as he had felt no guilt about the many other women he had seduced before Madge.

Yet, Gary also knew he was playing with fire. Each of the other women's husbands had never concerned him. OK, so he had been punched once by an irate husband as he clambered from the man's bed. And he had left the naked woman, whose name he couldn't even remember now, alone to face the angry man. He had almost broken his arm as he scurried out and hopped over the garden fence.

But Ken Tully was a different proposition altogether. Tully's reputation preceded him, and if the talk was anything to go by, this made him a very dangerous man. Storey had vowed to stay well clear of Tully.

Tully had no concern about the road being blocked. He knew these forests like the back of his hand. And if he started out now, he could make Cappawhite before midnight. He glared across the dark windswept forest, the cold rain beating on to his tough, handsome face. Tully wasn't afraid of the dark forest. Since he was a young man, he had camped alone in some of the most frightening places imaginable. These places which were scary at night though, could become the most awesomely beautiful places by day. He and his father would go hunting and fishing in the forest. But this was before the accident...

Tully was young, only twelve years old when it happened—but he didn't want to think about it. There were too many memories that caused him so much hurt, and so he had tried to erase them from his mind. But sometimes, like now, the damn memories just wouldn't go away.

Anyway, Tully didn't believe in ghosts or ghouls. He always believed that there was a perfectly good scientific explanation for everything. Yet, at night, when the nocturnal hunters came out, and the screams of the dying animals could be heard for miles around as they filled the night air—then the forest could feel scary. *No, the forests at night are no place for the faint hearted*, he reckoned.

Tully was about an hour into his journey, when he suddenly felt the cold around him increase immensely as the wind blew stronger. The trees and bushes shook violently in the darkness, and Tully couldn't remember ever seeing it this bad.

In the distance, he detected something up front. *A large deer,* he thought. It stood across the gap between two trees, unmoving, barely showing up in the moonlight. Tully had hunted deer in the past, and it puzzled him that as he neared the beast, it stood its ground as if waiting for him.

Deer were finely tuned animals with the most acute senses nature could have supplied. They possessed super sensitive hearing and smell, and Tully had never known one to let a man get as close as he was now.

*I am only fifteen to twenty feet away,* he thought. *Never! Perhaps it's caught in a trap. Or badly wounded from some hunter's badly aimed shot.* Tully stood and stared at it for a moment. *Maybe it has simply died in this position and stayed like this after death.*

Then it slowly moved, and immediately Tully saw that it was not a deer. The large hooded figure was about eight feet tall. It had risen up from a hunched position. As it straightened itself, its head moved from side to side. Then, it hissed.

Its back was toward him, and Tully instinctively ducked behind a tree. He held his breath. He didn't know what it was, but his instinct and fear told him not to move.

It rose about thirty feet up into the air on his left, and levitated out from between the trees. It was looking in his direction, and when it opened its mouth rows of black, shark-like teeth showed. Tully almost fell to his knees, but instead he gripped the bark of the tree tightly, dug his fingers in, and held on.

The creature seemed to sniff the air, as it swung its head from side to side in small, jerking movements. Then suddenly, it moved quickly off. Tully watched in fear, unmoving, as it disappeared into a clump of trees about two hundred yards away. Tully thought about the group of policemen that had been killed and the fact that the army were involved in a search for the perpetrator. He somehow knew that the murders were tied to this grotesque, flying creature.

Tully moved quickly on, not noticing that he still had the bunch of flowers held tightly in his grasp. Every ten feet or so he would stop and look around, praying that the creature would not see him. His heart pumped faster now, and for once in his life, he knew the meaning of real fear. It only took about thirty seconds of his forty-two years of life, to convince him that everything he had believed in before was wrong. Now science was not the explanation for everything, unless the real explanation was that he himself had gone insane.

Then Tully thought he heard a voice. He dived onto the ground, scrambling into some thick foliage.

Suddenly the voices were right beside him. "But I did see someone, sarge," the voice whispered.

"Maybe it was a Bigfoot?" someone else said, and laughed.

"Ok you two, shut it now and pay bloody attention," ordered the sergeant.

*Soldiers,* Tully thought. He was about to jump up and declare himself to these men, but he was afraid of being shot. So he stayed silent and still.

Tully reckoned there were about nineteen or twenty soldiers about him. Then they were gone, as quickly as they had come. Just as he was about to get up from the cold, wet ground, he noticed the flowers he had bought for Madge had been trampled underfoot. The petals were broken and squashed.

Suddenly the hooded figure passed over-head, moving fast, cape blowing in the wind, and he glared after it. It hadn't noticed him, and he knew why.

"The soldiers," Tully whispered. Then he heard machine gun and small arms fire. It was only about sixty or seventy yards away, and he could see the muzzle flashes. A salvo of rounds raked across the trees behind him, cutting through branches and tearing off large clumps of bark.

He dived once more to the ground and listened to the screams of dying men as the gunfire waned. The shooting stopped. Another few screams later, and it was all over.

The silence that followed was as unnatural as the creature had been, and Tully remained still. He saw it in the distance, coming his way, and he buried his head into the ground and prayed. He could taste the soil in his mouth and nose, but he tried not to breathe or even move a finger. A shadow moved over him, but he dared not bat an eyelid. Tully stayed perfectly still. He wasn't sure how long he had lay face down in the dirt. It may have only been a few minutes, but those minutes seemed like hours. Finally he knew he had to move. If he stayed like this, on the cold wet ground, he would be dead soon from hypothermia anyway.

Forcing himself up, Tully rubbed his stiff legs. He looked around at everything. There was no sign of the beast, and he felt sure it had passed him and had gone. He bravely made his way to where the shooting had come from. Tully couldn't believe the sight before him. He threw up almost instantly. He had gutted deer, rabbits, hares, and every other edible creature that had roamed the forest. Why, Tully had seen the things most people don't ever get to see outside of television and the comfort of their favourite armchairs. This though was different. These almost unrecognisable lumps of flesh scattered everywhere, with bits of military uniforms stuck to them, were once living, thinking men. Men with emotions and personalities. Men with mothers and fathers, with wives or girlfriends, and perhaps, even small children.

Tully cried softly for a moment. Then he trampled on through the rough grassland, away from the nightmare. He had been walking for about an hour through the increasing wind and rain, when he came to a clearing;

This was a very dangerous situation. Even the animals, Tully knew, were reluctant to move across open ground at night where all sorts of flying creatures could swoop down on them. He had to be very careful here. Tully glanced around at every bush and tree, before stealthily moving from the relative safety of the trees.

Suddenly a voice boomed out as a light shone onto his face, temporarily blinding him.

"Halt, who are you?" the voice ordered.

Suddenly he was surrounded by uniformed men, all armed. He noticed that one of the men wore the rank of a captain.

"I'm Tully," he answered.

"Cuff him," someone ordered, and Tully was pushed roughly up against a tree and searched.

"Found a Knife, sir," a private shouted back.

Tully was handcuffed and roughly pushed across the open ground until he was face to face with the captain.

"What were you doing with this knife?" the captain asked, as he stared at the small sheathed knife.

"I'm the gamekeeper at Tipperary, and I always carry a knife," Tully answered.

The captain stared accusingly at him, unconvinced.

"Look, my name's Tully. Go and check it out," he added.

"What are you doing in the woods at this time of night, Mr Tully?" the captain asked.

Tully didn't want to tell the man that he was going to Cappawhite to find the wife that had left him.

"I am looking for some poachers, hunting out of season," he lied.

The captain had never seen a gamekeeper dressed like Tully and immediately became suspicious. Why the man was wearing a suit, complete with tie, and polished brogue shoes, even though there was some mud on them. His trousers were grass-stained, and he had no rifle or shotgun with him.

"Take this man back to the village and let the police talk to him," the captain ordered.

"Wait, you're in great danger here," Tully pleaded, and pointed awkwardly with his cuffed wrists. "The other soldiers, way back in the forest, they're all dead. Killed by a bloody demon. I seen it, and if you go into that forest, it will kill every fucking one of you."

The young soldiers stared at each other for a moment, fear in their eyes. The captain ordered someone to contact the other patrol.

"There's no one alive to contact, damn you, you're too late," Tully yelled at him.

The captain was agitated now, and unsure of what to make of this man, "I would advise you to be quiet Mr Tully. You are frightening the younger men here."

"Well they'll be more than frightened if this creature shows up. They'll be bloody hamburger. Its strength knows no bounds—it's merciless," Tully exclaimed.

"Well then please answer me something would you? Just how the hell did you survive this massacre you witnessed first hand, without a scratch on you?" the captain asked Tully as he stared into his face.

Tully paused for a moment before speaking. "I hid," he said, head bowed, ashamed. "I hid."

# CHAPTER 9

Dan Winters pulled up at the house and worked over in his mind what he was going to tell Beatrice. He had arranged for his younger sister Betty to stay with her for a few days, and any days extra if need be. But he was afraid of what Beatrice's attitude to the younger girl would be. Dan just did not want Beatrice to be ignorant to Betty, or perhaps even violent, which she could be prone to being, and so he would have to run it passed her first, to see how she would react.

As he entered the hallway, three things told him that something wasn't right here. The house was in darkness, it was cold and there was no sound. Beatrice would never sit alone in the dark, and never in these almost freezing like temperatures.

Then Dan switched on the light and the note on the table was the first thing he noticed. It was short and sweet, but it said a thousand words as he dropped it onto the floor and ran into the bedroom. Beatrice's wardrobe was completely empty, and Dan was stunned. Then he slowly walked downstairs and slumped, head in hands, into the chair. The note had read…

Dan,

I have tried to tell you how I felt a million times, but you just would not listen. I no longer have any feelings for you. I'm going to live with my brother, Philip.

Don't act at all surprised. You knew this was coming, as I have tried to tell you so many times before. And don't come looking for me or there will be big trouble.

Beatrice


*Why has she done this?* Dan thought. *Haven't I washed, cooked, cleaned, and done every damn thing I could around the place to try and make her happy?* He could not even take leave from work now, because the risk of losing his job would have been too great.

Alright, so Dan hadn't loved Beatrice as much as Lynn, but he had still loved her—enough to want to stay with her the rest of his life. And if she only had shown some damn respect for him, then maybe he could have grown to love her more. Who knows what could have happened? He knew the note was final though, knew he wouldn't see her again. He felt sick for himself and disgusted with her.

Dan looked across at the little porcelain poodle that glared at him from the other side of the room, and thought back.

*Dan and Beatrice had been on their honeymoon in Paris. As they strolled, arm in arm along the Champs-Élysées, on that sunny afternoon; they stopped to look in a small shop window. Beatrice admired A little dog in the shop window, a very expensive little dog. At the time, Dan had said that it was much too costly, and Beatrice had walked off in a sulk. Although Beatrice was beautiful, there was a side to her Dan didn't like. She was a spoiled child, who had grown in to a spoiled adult and didn't cope well when things didn't go her way. Dan made some excuse the next day though to sneak out, and go buy it for her.*

*Dan didn't mention the poodle again, but slipped it into his luggage. His intent was to give it to her when they arrived home, as a surprise. But Beatrice sulked on the plane for the whole return journey. It wasn't until they had landed that he found out the huff was all because she thought he hadn't bought the poodle for her. When Dan finally gave her the damn poodle, the moment was already gone, and it ended as an embarrassment for both of them.*

Now Dan walked across and picked up the little ornamental poodle and gently cradled it.

"Guess you and I just weren't good enough my little friend," he said, as the tears rolled off his cheeks. He dropped down again into a chair and hugged the little porcelain dog.

Donald O'Shea was collating papers in the police station, when they received the call from the Army unit. E-Patrol was not answering any calls, and they had arrested someone in the forest.

"Have you identified the person yet?" Donald asked into the microphone.

"He says his name is Tully," came the reply.

Sergeant McCann stepped in.

"I know Tully, Sir," he said to Donald. "He's a gamekeeper from Tipperary Town. Why Tully knows the bloody forest like the back of his hand. He's a good man, and we could really use his help on this."

"Return to the station, and bring the priso… um, Tully with you," Donald corrected. "And don't hurt him," he added.

It was nearly an hour later when the patrol returned to the little station in Cappawhite, and an overwrought Tully had to be calmed down.

"What right do you fucking people have to arrest me?" Tully yelled angrily.

Donald gently took Tully to one side, and sat down at a very large table, that seemed out of place in the small room. But Tully refused to sit down and stood firm.

"Tell me what happened out there tonight, Mr Tully," Donald asked.

"Forget the mister. It's just Tully," he answered.

99

"And I'll tell you what happened. A fucking demon came down from the trees and killed all those poor young men in about ten fucking seconds. Left their bodies scattered in pieces all over the bloody place. That's what happened! I don't care if you believe me or not, but I witnessed it. I've tried to tell him this, but this sad excuse for an officer..."

Donald called Sergeant McCann over to the table, interrupting Tully, and bade him to sit down again. He gently held Tully's arm as he did so.

"I'm Superintendent Donald O'Shea, and this is Sergeant Blair McCann," he whispered.

"Yes, I know Blair. I know Blair very well," Tully answered.

"Then Blair has something to tell you, Tully."

"Please, Tully, why don't you just sit down?" Blair said as he pointed to the chair.

Tully finally deigned to sit in the chair, and then held up his manacled hands.

"Uncuff this man," Donald ordered.

Within seconds, Tully was rubbing his freed wrists. Blair leaned across the table toward him, and spoke softly, just out of earshot from the other men in the room.

"The Superintendent and I both believe you, Tully, because as young constables we both came face to face with this creature—many years ago. We know what you saw, and we know what it can do, because we also witnessed its strength!"

"Then what, in Gods good name, is it then?" Tully asked.

For the next hour the two policemen told Tully everything they knew about the creature, about Otis and the other stories and legends they had been told. After they stopped talking, an awkward silence filled the room. Tully volunteered to help them, and cited his knowledge of the forest and his ability to track nearly anything that moved.

"I received a call from America," Donald added. "A man by the name of 'Dan Winters' called. He is flying over tomorrow. He's a reporter from LA, and it seems Sarah Tweedy wrote to him before she died…"

"So Sarah is dead then?" Blair interrupted.

"Yes, and this Winters fella just might have some real information that could help us here."

"I'll organise lodgings for him at the Ross Inn," Blair offered.

*The Ross Inn,* Tully thought. *This is why I came here in the first place.*

"If I'm not under arrest, can I go?" Tully asked. "I will be back to help you in the morning. I promise!"

"By all means," Donald answered. "You're not a prisoner here, Tully."

Tully informed the men he would see them early next day, shook hands, and left.

The Ross Inn was only two hundred yards from the police station, but the place was swathed in total darkness as Tully approached. *Damn,* he thought, *one o'clock in the bloody morning. Madge will be asleep by now.* Tully knew his wife would normally go to bed long before midnight.

Tully moved around the back of the old, four story building and climbed the fire escape. He had to go all the way to the top before he could find an open door. He felt like a burglar, and knew if he were caught, he would be charged as one.

Entering into the dark hallway Tully tiptoed along the corridor and down the large staircase. A small pilot light partly lit up the hall and he could just make out a tiny counter with some leaflets on top, a telephone, and a large guest book. His heart beat faster in anticipation of seeing his wife again. Yet he knew it wouldn't be easy trying to persuade her to come home with him.

Tully sat down on the floor, behind the counter and pulled a small torch from his pocket. He shone the little torch onto the pages, but he had trouble making out most of the bad handwriting in the guest book. There were no signatures. He squinted hard as he turned the pages.

Going back to the date Madge had left him, Tully felt his heart beat even faster as he realised there were no women registered as staying here alone during this period. It was a couple of minutes later, just as the little torch started to flicker, that he came upon the names 'Mr and Mrs G Storey.' It was right there, bold as you please. Slap bang in the centre of the register column, staring out at him. The realisation of it all immediately tore at his insides. He knew Gary Storey, not very well, but as the Bingo caller at the hall back in Tipperary. Storey also had a reputation as a womaniser. Tully now knew what was going on, and felt like the largest fool in the world: Tully felt betrayed.

Tully's father wandered into his mind again, like he often did when his mind was troubled. This time Tully couldn't shake him off.

*His father with the James Dean looks had only been promoted to supervisor two days before the fire at the paint factory. Three men had been trapped in a storeroom, and his brave, foolhardy father had placed a wet towel over his head and ran in to try and save them. He only managed to get two of the men out, and was going back for the third, when the roof collapsed. The man left inside the storeroom was killed. His father had only just managed to survive, staggering to safety at the last minute. But he paid a terrible price—his face, chest and arms had been very badly burned, and he was hospitalised for over a year. The injuries to his face were grotesque, and his mother just couldn't accept him any more. After this, his father moved into the spare room and hardly ever came out, except to eat and use the bathroom.*

*One day Tully came home early from school and heard the sounds of a blazing argument in progress.*

*'I don't want you any more!' his mother had shouted at his father. 'Why don't you just go away from us? It would have been better if you'd died in the fire.'*

*His father had grabbed his gear and ran into the woods, crying. This brave man, who had saved the lives of others, would never return.*

*Tully would never look at his mother the same way again. He learned to hate her for her selfishness, and her cruelty. How could any woman do that to such a brave man like his father?*

Tully searched for years to try and find his father. He had visited all their favourite spots, but it wasn't until many years later that that he finally found him.

Lamont's Mine, so called because of the man who first started digging there, was only about fifty or sixty meters deep. The old copper mine had been abandoned shortly after mining operations had started. Tully remembered his father's explanation of why. The men working the mine had witnessed something strange there. something frightening, enough to abandon their digging, and never return. Word soon spread, and no one ever worked there again. His father had made him promise he would never go near Lamont's Mine. The boy had wholeheartedly obeyed, frightened at the horrors his father had told him.

Many years later when Tully was twenty years old, he was coming home from a fishing trip; when he had his own encounter at Lamont's mine. He had heard a voice that sounded like his old neighbour, Mr Maguire. Apparently, Maguire's dog had run off and the old man had gone into the forest to try and find him. Tully followed the pitiful cries for help and somehow ended up outside of Lamont's Mine. Then he heard Mr Maguire's voice from inside. Despite all warnings, the old man had still, bravely decided to go in after his dog.

As Tully entered the mine, the first thing that struck him was the cold. Freezing it was, and the echo of the dogs whimpering scared him all the more.

"Come out, Mr Maguire!" Tully said in a low voice, but the sound echoed back and forward.

"Come out, Mr Maguire!" It echoed mockingly like it was bouncing off a thousand cavern walls. "Come out, come out, come out..."

Tully was really frightened. He bravely shone his torch light around the desolate, frigid man-made cave, with the rotted wooden beams projecting out from all angles.

Something suddenly fluttered behind him, and then rammed into the back of his head. He caught it in the fading beam of the torch, just as it flew away. A bat! It flew off, deeper into the mine. As he moved the beam of light down and across the floor, he saw the dog. The animal was pawing at a large bundle on the floor.

As soon as Tully neared the dog—he knew that the bundle laying there was his father's remains. He recognised the old, red-chequered windbreaker, the one his father always had worn, and, though they had faded badly, his yellow leather gloves. Tully also realised from the position of the 7mm hunting rifle, and the shattered skull, exactly what his father had done. His father knew no one went into Lamont's mine, and that no one would think of looking for him here, especially his son. So he had deliberately ended his life inside this place.

Fighting back tears, Tully grabbed the dog by the collar to keep it with him. Then he yelled again for Mr Maguire.

"I'm in here," the weak man's voice answered.

Braving the next chamber of the mine, Tully finally found the old man. Maguire had hunkered down behind a fallen support beam, and was shaking.

"I think there's something down here, and it isn't just bats" he said in a shaky voice.

Tully thought he sensed a movement, somewhere deeper into the mine. So he roughly pulled Mr Maguire to his feet, and the two of them high-tailed it out of the mine, followed by the dog.

Tully had cried for days after this over the death of his father and the purist evil he had felt in Lamont's mine. Yet, he bravely accompanied the constables and some volunteers to retrieve his father's remains from the cave. Days later, his mother confirmed Tully's worst opinions of her when she refused to go to the funeral.

Tully rationalised that deep down, he had always known that his father was dead. He knew his father would never have deserted him like that. And despite being a strong and vital man, he just couldn't handle the emotional scars that his injuries had placed upon him. He simply wanted to die.

Tully remembered his fathers sob's, coming from his lonely room at night, begging for God to take him. Sometimes alone in his room, Tully would cry along with him.

Now, Tully reluctantly accepted that his father had only needed a small push to drive him over the edge. Nothing filled the void in Tully's life after his father left, and as he grew up, he became sullen and withdrawn. He even stopped talking to anyone for a time.

Tully had grown to hate his mother even more after his father first left. He suffered a constant barrage of abuse. The slightest thing would set her off. She would scream, and yell at him, and sometimes she would beat him with a leather strap. The strap hurt less than the screaming, threats, and name calling.

"You're just like your lazy, no good father. You can do for everyone else, but never do anything right for your own bloody family," she had yelled at him one afternoon and hurled a kitchen skillet as his head.

"Just like your lazy, no good father" was a compliment to Tully. *If I can ever be half the man my father was,* he thought, *then I will go through life with a smile on my face.*

When Tully's mother died the young man attended her funeral, but with no sense of loss or sorrow. He really couldn't understand how he could feel this way toward the woman who had given him birth. He tried hard to think back when he was really young. He had loved her then. Back then, when they had been a loving family that did things together. *How things can change,* Tully thought. Tully knew this was part of life, but people were usually kinder to each other, got through the bad times and became stronger for it. Yet his mother had not. Her heart was hollow and void, and so she could no longer feel anything for his father, get past his injuries and love him for the man he was. So Tully laid all the blame squarely on her, and nothing would ever change that for him.

During the funeral, several members of the family approached him to say how sorry they were for his loss. Tully thanked them sombrely, and then brusquely walked away. He didn't even pretend to put on a show of grief. Only his father filled his thoughts during his mother's funeral, and although God may have forgiven her for what she did, he never would.

# CHAPTER 10

Dan plopped himself down in the uncomfortable, plastic seat and placed his small suitcase beside him. As he waited for the check-in to open, he wiped away some tears that were forming in his eyes. A little boy with a large yellow balloon pulled at Dan's trouser leg, and he smiled at the boy. He was about to ask the child his name when the boys mother stormed over like a raging bull and roughly pulled the protesting child away.

*Telling the child not to talk to strangers, was one thing,* Dan thought. *But this was instilling hatred and mistrust for people that the young boy may never get over.* He looked sadly at the child. Dan thought of how different Beatrice might have been, if she had been able to have children. But that blessing had been denied to them, and he tried to erase the thought from his mind.

Dan didn't realise that his innocent glance at the boy had now turned into a stare. Suddenly the child's' mother was once again standing in front of him.

"Pervert," she mouthed, as she pulled the child away for the second time.

Dan reddened slightly, even though he knew he had done nothing wrong. The world was often a sick place, and maybe this lady was just over protective toward her child. Then his thoughts wandered back to

Beatrice again, and he buried his head in his hands. He hadn't wanted his marriage to end like this, not after the fifteen years they had spent together. But, just like this incident, he was being made out to be a villain here. It just wasn't fair.

*You try to do the right thing, and what does it get you? Nothing!* he thought.

Trying to distract himself, Dan removed Sarah's letter from his briefcase. He went over it again and again, making sure he had not missed any details. He had though, committed most of it to memory.

An announcement over the loudspeaker informed the passengers of a delay on the Air Lingus flight to Ireland, but Dan was no longer listening. He was so engrossed in the page that he had heard nothing. The piece he was reading about, informed him that Otis had gone to America to search out an ex-partner, Eric Little Feather. Little Feather was a full-blooded Lakota Sioux who lived at the Isabella Indian reservation at the time. One of the details that Sarah had related was that Otis had chanted a Native American phrase as he fought the beast.

Otis had also taken notes, written on a pad from his hotel room. The notes had been found in his bag after his death. The account told of the events when Otis went to visit the old medicine man, Joseph Lapahie, and also mentioned he had been accompanied by another man, Peter Ahenekaw. Better still, an address for Joseph Lapahie had been written down.

Dan moved quickly from his seat and phoned his boss at the paper. This was something he needed to do first, before he travelled across to Ireland. Something important! He must see if he could find either Joseph Lapahie or Peter Ahenekaw. They may just have some more additional information that could help him.

Just as Dan was returning to the waiting area, a large, heavy man appeared. He was panting slightly and he looked agitated. He was accompanied by the woman who had accosted Dan earlier.

"Shit," Dan said, under his breath.

"Is this the guy?" the red-faced man said.

"Yes, Elmer, that's him," she answered and pointed at Dan.

"Step outside here, you damn faggot," he hollered at Dan as he pointed to the barrier. "Let's see just what your scrawny ass is made off."

"Listen, your wife's got it all wrong pal. I did nothing wrong here. I simply said hello to the child," Dan pleaded.

"You a-callin' my wife a liar, boy?" the man croaked. He was now waving his large fists about in an aggressive manner.

"Why no, I'm simply saying she's mistaken."

"No Elmer, he had this look. You know the one I mean," the woman said.

Protest as he might, Dan knew this guy was itching for a fight. He also knew that no matter what he said this guy wasn't going to listen.

"Why I'm gonna bust your damn ass!" the man threatened.

"Kick his ass, Elmer, its' the only damn way that his kind learns," the woman stated.

Dan turned to walk away, but the man, continuously urged on by the woman, lunged at him. Dan, was too quick though, and spun on his heels, catching the man cleanly on the chin with a left hook. Thus the fight had ended as quickly as it begun, and

Dan walked away. The man was laid out cold on the ground, and the woman's obscenities still echoed in his ears.

Back in Ireland, Tully stared at the room number and felt his heart sink. *Legs eleven*, he thought. Tully wondered why this phrase was going through his head as he made his way back upstairs. He approached the door to room eleven and held his ear to it, but could hear nothing from inside. Then he furiously kicked the door open and burst into the large, sparsely furnished room.

The couple on the bed immediately sat up. Madge gave out a yell, while Storey, who was naked, tried to run out the door. Tully caught the man with an uppercut to his chin, and sent him flying backward across the bed.

"Leave him alone, you bastard," his wife shouted as he went to strike the unconscious man for a second time.

"So this is why you left me?" Tully shouted. "For this scum?" He stared threateningly at the limp man, who was unmoving and breathing in gasps. Blood trickled from Storey's lips.

Suddenly there were other people in the room, and the landlady instructed someone to call the police.

"Who are you and what are you doing here?" The landlady bellowed.

"Sh-she-is my-my wife," Tully groaned, pointing a shaking hand at the distraught woman. He fell down into the only chair in the room, head in his hands.

Soon three policemen, led by Sergeant McCann, arrived and entered the room.

"Tully," he said, surprised as he saw him. McCann then glanced across at the naked man, unconscious on the bed. "What the hell's going on here?"

"Blair, this man says that this woman is his wife," answered the landlady.

The sergeant now recognised Madge Tully, who was now sobbing loudly on the bed. McCann had no sympathy for Storey. He had known the man's reputation and all the trouble this man has caused over the years. But it was Tully who had committed the offence here, and by law, McCann would have to act on it.

After arresting Tully, McCann made sure that the victim, who had since come around, was alright. He then took Tully down to accompany him on the short walk to the police station.

One of the older constables turned to Storey as Tully was removed from the room and spoke sharply to him.

"Shame on you, son," he said, wagging a finger at Storey. "Shame on you," he repeated.

When they entered the station, Donald could not believe that Tully was now standing before him in such a broken state. He had spoken to the man and asked for his help, a mere half-hour before. Now here he was, being booked and with blood on his fist. Donald shook his head and walked slowly into another room.

*So that was why Tully was in the woods at night, dressed like he was going out to a dinner party,* Donald thought. *He was chasing down his wife.*

Now though, Tully's world had been turned on its head, and Donald knew from his police experience that only more time would heal this man. He would try to talk to him in the morning, and knock some sense into him. This matter was bigger than Tully. Bigger than all of them! This was now about the many innocent civilians who might lose their lives before this situation could be brought under control.

But Donald needed as much help as he could get. Donald needed Tully!

Back at the Ross Inn, Storey had decided he had had enough and packed his belongings. Madge cried and begged him not to go. He had been humiliated by Tully, and badly injured. He just wasn't prepared for a damn repeat performance.

Storey had had already met someone else. About three weeks previously, the old landlady's daughter, Vera, had come on strong to him, and he had been meeting the naive girl at every opportunity. Only yesterday she had coaxed him to run away with her. So now that was exactly what he planned to do.

*Beside,* Storey thought, *I'm the one footing the bill here, and it's starting to put a serious drain on my finances. At least Vera managed to produce a nice little wad when I asked her about money. Probably stole it from her mother, and been squirreling it away for a while. It's a nice big wad, too. Probably keep us going for a while. At least, it'll do until something or someone else crops up.*

Storey sat one week's board money on the dressing table. After that, Madge would be on her own. He was convinced Tully would take her back anyway, regardless of their little affair. Madge would be alright. So as far as he was concerned, his conscience was clear.

Storey packed quickly, and then walked out, rubbing his jaw. "Goodbye, Madge," he said and slammed the door without looking back. He walked down the two flights to Vera's room in the basement and knocked.

Madge just lay on the bed, unmoving, and sobbed uncontrollably.

"I love you," said Vera as Storey drove at speed from Cappawhite, and she held his arm tightly.

"And I love you, my love," he answered. Storey's jaw still ached, but it made it easier not to smirk when he told her what he knew she wanted to hear.

Soon they were out in the countryside, driving along the dark rain-soaked roads in the middle of the night.

Vera leaned across the seat, pulling herself closer to him. "Mother says there's a murderer on the loose out here," she said, frightened.

"Well now, don't you worry about that. I won't let any harm come to you. He'll be taking on the wrong fella if he tries anything with me," Storey bragged and made a swipe with his fist.

Vera felt secure, and squeezed his arm. With her strong, new man at her side, the fear soon left her.

They were about four miles from Cappawhite when a large fox suddenly bolted from the hedge in front of them. Storey instinctively pulled at the wheel, swerving to avoid it. But it was too late as the sound of an almighty thud came from the front of the car, and they skidded to a stop.

The fox, bloodied and mangled had caught itself in the front grill. Although torn and badly injured, it struggled violently to break free. Vera closed her eyes and looked away as this desperate animal fought for its life. It pushed and half-climbed onto the front of the bonnet, face bloodied. It scratched and writhed, and its dark eyes seemed to take one last accusing look at Vera, as death finally overtook it.

Storey opened the trunk and looked for something to pry the dead fox from the grill. Then as he walked back to the front, tyre lever in hand, a sudden movement caught his eye. It was the large fox, and it wasn't dead. Somehow it had finally managed to free itself. Now, it was crawling slowly along the side of the road, gasping and choking for breath, leaving a sickening trail of blood and gore in its wake.

With one unnatural and grotesque movement, the fox suddenly twisted its body. It twisted around toward Storey, and bared its bloodied teeth. Storey stepped back, afraid. Then in another weird motion, the fox turned its head away from him, looking upward, seeming to watch something behind him.

Storey nervously looked over his shoulder, as the fox continued to stare at the movement in the tree tops. Storey saw nothing in the darkness, but he heard the branches as they swayed fiercely in the wind, bending and creaking.

"Let's get the hell out of here," Vera's voice rang out.

"Wait," Storey answered as he tried to focus on the distant trees. Then he saw it, faintly, moving high up in the branches and at some distance away. It was a large, floating figure. This made him even more frightened than before.

"C'mon, Gary, please, lets get out of here," Vera repeated.

Storey turned and hurried to the car door. He didn't noticing that the fox, its tongue protruding from its mouth, now lay dead.

Vera whimpered as she pointed behind him. "L-l-look," she stuttered.

Storey could see the hooded figure clearly, coming toward them. His jaw no longer ached, but dropped in fright. He moved to the rear of the car, before sprinting off into the night. He heard Vera's voice somewhere behind him, as she screamed and shouted for him.

"Come back, come back," she pleaded, but on he ran, until her voice was just a fading whisper, way back in the distance.

Vera reached across and frantically pulled the driver's door closed. She locked each door in turn, and tightly closed her open window.

But all these actions were in vain. It was upon her, pressing its grotesque face against her window. It opened its mouth, revealing the rows of sickening, black teeth. The large yellow tongue licked at the glass, leaving streaks of slime oozing down the panes. Vera fainted as it rubbed the dead fox's bloodied head against her window. Then it wailed loudly.

It was only about three and a half miles now to Cappawhite, and Storey continued to run as fast as his legs would take him. He didn't care what happened to Vera, or how she fared now that he left her alone. The only thing that moved him was the horrifying wail that echoed across the dark forest sky.

Storey prayed and begged the Lord to let him live. He would never bother with married women again, he promised God. He would attend church every week and endeavour to spend the rest of his life working for the Lord. If only God would let him live through this, and spare him from this monster.

Storey could see a faint light, a building, far off in the distance. He started praying aloud, panting for breath as he ran on. He felt someone there would help him, if only he could reach it in time.

Suddenly, there was a movement, high up in the branches of the trees near him. Storey stopped and slowly moved to the side of the road. He looked desperately in all directions. He had seen the beast float through the trees, coming for them at the car, watched the fox's unnatural movements…

Storey felt something, his trousers suddenly wet and cold. *God*, he thought, *I've pissed my bloody self.* He hunkered down beside the hedge. Sweat now rolled from his brow, even in the cold of the night. He continued to whisper short, almost incoherent prayers to himself.

The silence was intense now and after five minutes, Storey concluded that the beast hadn't chased him after all. It was busy killing the girl, whose name at this moment he couldn't even remember. Self-preservation was his only concern now. He didn't care if he was behaving like the mother of all cowards. He wanted to live, and to hell with everyone else.

Then something moved again, high to his right.

It was here!

*Oh God*, he thought, *it has found me.*

Storey bit hard on his finger and crouched down even lower now. His breathing was sporadic, and his hands shaking. He had been offered the chance to leave Ireland a few years ago, when his brother immigrated to Australia, but he turned the opportunity down. Now he was sorry. Storey swore that if he ever got out of this mess that he would waste no time in writing to his brother and make arrangements to go live there.

*Anywhere would be better than this shit hole of a place,* he thought. He was sure he heard a twig snap behind the hedge and cowered down until he was almost touching the ground.

Storey didn't see the large gnarled hand come through the bottom of the hedge and grip his ankle tightly. Then, with a single, quick movement, he was pulled forcefully through the hedge, screaming. A plume of broken twigs and small leaves flew high into the night air.

Storey didn't even feel himself being dragged deep into the dark forest. Mercifully, he blacked out before he even got a chance to see the creature close up.

All that remained of the hedge was a large gapping hole and evidence of some torn roots. All over the forest, there was an eerie silence.

# CHAPTER 11

Dan sat on a small plane that would take him inland to the Isabella Indian reservation, and to Joseph Lapahie's last known address. He had read Otis's notes, and he guessed that the old Indian was most probably dead by now. But Dan needed the answers to some important questions before he went to Ireland, and he felt sure someone there could help him.

Dan got lucky and was quickly able to get a cab at the airport. He gave the cab driver Lapahie's address and was at the house in less than forty five minutes.

A large worn out brass knocker of an Indian chief adorned the front door, but instead of rapping it, Dan pressed the brightly lit door bell. He was about to buzz again, when the door opened and an old, large and immaculately dressed Indian woman answered.

It took Dan five minutes to explain exactly why he was there. Once the woman was satisfied with his explanation, he was cordially invited inside.

An extremely tall man, with a large nose approached him in the hallway and shook hands. "Hello," he said smiling, and Dan flinched at the strong mans firm grip. "Sit down and make yourself at home. My name is Thomas, Thomas Lapahie. The Joseph Lapahie you seek was my grandfather. So you have come to find out about the Great Spirit Woman? Sit down and we shall talk some."

Dan had hardly time to say thank you as Thomas ushered him into a large wicker chair that had seen better days. The room itself was packed with Native American artefacts, which Dan guessed were worth a lot of money.

Thomas Lapahie spoke affectionately, and at length about the man who had raised him. He also related the story of how his own father was sent to death row for a murder that he didn't commit. It was clear to Dan that this man had been very close to his grandfather.

"I remember when the big, black fella with the scarred face came to see grandfather. The one you call 'Otis.' He gave me twenty dollars when he visited. I was eight years old then, but I remember his visit very clearly. No one ever gave me that kind of money before," Thomas said. "His wife was in big trouble, and grandfather told him the things he needed to do. Grandfather told me some time later that Otis had been killed. He knew that Otis had not destroyed the creature, since it cannot be killed. He told me that the spirit woman wanted to take Otis's wife, and this was bad medicine. Sometimes grandfather and I would talk about the spirit woman. He told me other stories about people's encounters with the creature."

Thomas spent twenty minutes telling Dan the story about the Sioux warrior, Satra, who went out alone across the plains to meet the demon head on, so that no one else would be killed for him.

Then Thomas turned to another story. "I also remember the time he told me about the boat, a submarine boat."

"Submarine?" Dan asked, puzzled.

"Yes, I remember the story like it was yesterday. I even remember the number of the boat. It was U-301. It was sailing out in the middle of the Atlantic and…"

"How did your grandfather come across this story?" Dan interrupted.

"Grandfather knew an old German fisherman, Horst Steiner, who moved to America after the war. He was a young seaman on board U-301. I don't know how the conversation came about, but grandfather became friendly with Horst. He said Horst just came out with it one day, after they had been drinking together."

"And this story relates to this spirit woman?" Dan asked.

"Yes, do you wish to hear it?"

"Yeah, sure do," Dan answered. "I want to know everything there is about this damn creature."

"Then I will relay the story to you the way Horst told it to grandfather, and then the way Grandfather told it to me.

*Horst said they were patrolling the Atlantic for just over a week, and they had been depth charged twice in two days after sinking about two thousand tons of Allied shipping. The stale, claustrophobic conditions were starting to tell on the men and it was a great relief to them when the Captain gave the order to surface. Even*

*though the men knew how rough the sea was up top, no one cared.*

*Only the officers of the watch were allowed up onto the conning tower. But Captain Holtz had ordered that an extra two men at a time could go topside for ten minute durations.*

*The captain was sure that even a wet, cloudy sky and the grey windswept ocean, would at least give the men a change of scenery. It would almost certainly help their morale. Besides, ten minutes on the conning tower with the wind and rain lashing into their faces would make them quite happy to go below again, where it was dry and secure.*

*They were on the surface for only about ten minutes when Vergal, one of the lookouts, spotted what he thought was a plane, faintly in the distance.*

*'Captain,' he called, and Holtz looked out with his binoculars. 'We're too far from shore for it to be a land based aircraft, so there must be a carrier nearby,' Vergal stated.*

*'Prepare to dive,' the captain ordered.*

*'My God!' the lookout said.*

*'What is it, Vergal?' the captain asked.*

*But Vergal could only stare at him with an open mouth.*

*The captain looked quickly up again with his binoculars, and repeated Vergal's, My God!' Then he shouted at the men beside him, 'Alaaaaaarm! Alaaaaaarm!'*

*The siren blared out its deafening clang, and in no time, the men had scurried down below. Vergal was in a state of shock as he tried to tell the men what he had seen. But the captain was too busy pulling the hatch shut to even think about the hooded figure he had witnessed descending rapidly toward them.*

*The hatch was about three-quarters closed when the large, gnarled hand pushed its way into the gap and effortlessly pulled it open again. Then the creature came through, and levitated down into the boat as water started to pour into the sub as it dove.*

*'Surface, surface!' the captain yelled, lest they all drown.*

*The sailors fought with the blow out valves, the pneumatics struggling to force the flood tanks free of enough water to allow them to rise. Suddenly the water stopped pouring in as the vessel resurfaced.*

*Then the captain ordered two of the sailors to equip themselves with firearms. The creature slowly and frighteningly hovered in the midst of the men.*

*Moving its head from side to side, the creature slowly turned around 360 degrees. The frightened men stood back as far as the hull plates, valves and gauges would allow them. There was no escape they knew, and whispered prayers were the only thing that broke the uncanny silence.*

*It opened its black lips, and hissed loudly at the sailors, before throwing its head back and seemingly sniffing at the air. Menacingly it moved forward, toward the bows section, then abruptly stopped. The creature started to shake, slowly at first, but this soon gave way to violent spasms. The creature's hood fell back revealing its grotesque face. Tufts of long, green hair fell from its grey-skinned head. Its red, narrow eyes were rolling in its head, and a black foam like substance ran from its horrendous lips, and the creature's many rows of teeth chattered violently.*

*Then its flesh started to peel off in small grey strips from its hands and face. The creature wailed in its pain, but it struggled on as it continued to try and make it to the front of the boat. It extended a large bony hand forward, reaching and shaking.*

*Two sailors appeared at the rear hatchway and opened fire on the beast with their Schmeisser machine pistols. Someone handed the captain his Lugar, and he quickly fired off into the beast's head.*

*Normally, it would have been unheard of to discharge any weapon in an enclosed space like a submarine—but these were not normal circumstances. If a few men were to be killed or injured for the sake of the crew at large, then the captain felt this was the price they would had to pay.*

*The creature turned and made for the outer hatch, its aim to get to the front of the boat, now abandoned. The ships mate, Reidel, a very strong man who once wrestled at the Games, was already on the steps, waiting. He was determined to block its path.*

*The captain screamed for Reidal to move away from the beast, but his voice was drowned out over the gunfire, and the creature's wailing. As it made for the hatchway, Reidal punched at its already torn face. The beast pulled the mate up by his legs in a match of strength the men had never witnessed before, and violently swung him round. Reidal's head exploded as it hit one of the ballast tank levers, spraying blood everywhere.*

*Then as another brave sailor tried to get hold of it, the creature effortlessly tore off his arm. Suddenly the lights went out, and in the red glare of the emergency lighting, men ran aft and forward in their panic. The armed sailors reloaded and continued to fire at the creature, but the ricocheting bullets struck another of their seamen. The captain, now out of ammunition, could only look helplessly on.*

*But the beast was suffering horribly now, and from some other unknown force, the captain believed. It was not being hurt by the bullets at all, he felt. Then in a flash, the creature struggled up and out through the upper hatchway, wailing as it went. Suddenly, it was gone, just as quickly as it had come.*

*A brave sailor climbed the steps and nervously, closed the hatch. The captain once again screamed for them to dive. The alarm sounded and the ship went sleekly beneath the waves, away from this thing, deep into the depths——to safety!*

*The captain stared down at Reidel, the brave mate, whose body was now being lifted carefully onto a stretcher. Reidel was his best friend from childhood, and Captain Holtz wept as he thought about them growing up together. Reidel had once fought three bullies at school that had threatened him, thrashing them with ease. He had seen Reidel wrestle before the war and he knew the strength the man possessed, but he had also witnessed this creature kill his brave friend with little or no effort. He understood the great strength the beast possessed.*

*The ship was operating on radio silence, and as Holtz staggered back to his quarters, he passed the distraught seamen who were visibly crying and in shock, and determined that a message would have to be sent out.*

*Going through the rear hatchway, the captain thought about how the creature had seemed determined to go forward, towards the bows of the boat. He was sure it had a purpose, and he paused at the opening for a moment.*

*'Rochel,' he said to one of the seamen,*

*'Yes, captain.'*

*'Get me a full list of all the men on duty, forward from this position.'*

*'Yes, Sir,' Rochel answered, puzzled.*

*About fifteen minutes later Rochel entered the captain's quarters.*

*'Here is the list you asked for, Sir,' he said and placed the list in the captains' hands.*

*The captain stared at the sheet of names without really looking at it, because he was really only interested in one name. And one name in particular stood out against the others—Bachmann!*

*Hans Bachmann had returned on board at Brest, and just in the nick of time, otherwise he would have been registered as absence without leave. When Bachmann came on board, he was immediately taken to sick bay. The captain was* assured that the man was not drunk, but in a state of shock. Rather than order him off the already delayed boat, Holtz ordered them under way. He wanted to avoid further delays, and he felt the statements and paper work involved were just not worth it.

In any case, Bachmann was one of his best crewmen, and he hoped that whatever was wrong with him, was only temporary. One of the medics had reported that Bachmann had been almost delirious on the first night of their journey and had been saying things in his sleep. Strange things. Things that had frightened Fritz, the youngest member of the crew. Then Bachmann's odd behaviour stopped, and two days later, he was back on duty again, as good as before. There was no hint that anything had ever been wrong with him.

The captain looked at the sheet before him, and verified again that the name was there.

'Send Bachmann to my quarters,' Holtz ordered.

'Right away, captain,' the sailor reply.

It was a full five minutes when Bachmann hesitantly entered the captain's quarters, and Holtz noticed immediately how the sailor fidgeted and nervously pulled at his cap.

'Sit down Hans, and relax,' he said. 'Have you heard what happened on board today?

'Yes, j-just this minute,' Hans stuttered. He sat down stiffly as if still at attention. His hands were shaking and his lips twitching.

The captain feared that this man was not at all back to his normal, confident self.

'*I am sorry I returned late to the ship, captain,*' *he said meekly.*

'*No Hans, you returned on time. Anyway, I am not interested in the time you returned, but I want to talk to you about the condition you returned in. Are you prepared to talk about it?*'

*Hans looked out into the open corridor, and then nervously back to the captain. Now he pulled at his cap even more than before.*

*The captain leaned across and tenderly held Bachmann's hands for a second. He looked kindly into the distraught sailor's eyes.*

'*Go on, Hans. You don't need to be afraid any longer,*' *he said.*

'*I-I don't know what you mean, Sir?*' *Hans stuttered.*

'*When you were in the sick bay, you talked of a Demon. Tell me about it now, Hans,*' *the captain urged.*

'*It must have been a nightmare, Sir, I was delirious. It was the fever perhaps?*'

'*Well, something came on board tonight. It killed the First Mate, and injured Hector and Johan. It was trying to get to the forward section, but something happened to it, and it left. Yet, I can assure you that it wasn't our weapons that drove it off. I need to know if this creature from hell is going to come back for you, Hans, because I think it was looking for you.*'

*Hans pushed his head into his hands and stifled a muffled cry.* '*Wh-what did it look like, captain,* Hans whispered. His eyes wide with fear.*

'It was grotesque. It was hooded when it came on board…'

'Oh God! No, please, it is looking for me. Oh God,' Hans said. He jumped up from the seat and leaned his head tightly against the bulkhead, crying.

'If you want me to help you then you must tell me about this thing,' the captain urged.

Hans sat slowly down again, and began to talk. He had not mentioned it earlier because he felt that no one on board would believe him, and he didn't want to be left open to ridicule.

He had met a girl at the Café Parrisiene, a girl named Mariana. They had gone for a walk in the nearby park, even though it was starting to get dark. He missed his wife and he only wanted some female company for a while. He knew he couldn't stay long with her though, because he had to return to the ship. But Mariana had been beautiful, and he had decided to stretch his time with her as far as he possibly could.

Hans had held her hand and the girl had responded by squeezing his tightly, and then they had kissed. It was a warm affectionate kiss, and probably the last one Hans would get for a while. He was very aware of the dangers a sub-mariner took every time he went to sea, but it was his duty, and not something he would dwell on.

It was Mariana who saw it first, after she opened her eyes as the kiss ended. She roughly pushed Hans back and pointed into the cloudless sky.

*Hans had backed away in terror as the monk like figure floated slowly down to them. He didn't even notice Mariana faint and slump onto the grass. Suddenly the figure was close to him, caressing his face for what seemed like an eternity. And then it was gone, as quickly as it had come. The incident had left him so shocked that he didn't even remember leaving the park or returning for duty.*

*'Please don't let it get to me, captain, please,' Bachmann pleaded, as he wiped away his tears that were streaming down his face.*

*The captain assured Bachmann that he was safe for now, and the man seemed to accept his word for it. The captain dismissed him and he nervously smiled, saluted, and walked promptly away.*

*Captain Holtz wasn't really so sure about Bachmann's safety. He stared solemnly at a painting of his submarine on the cabin wall for a moment, before walking briskly out into the main hatchway.*

*It was eight days later when U-301 returned to Brest. The crew left the boat in a subdued manner, rather than with the rowdy elation that usually comes from sailors coming into port.*

*As they filed up the small gangway, a fair-sized crowd cheered and shouted, almost drowning out the brass band that was playing an out of tune version of the William Tell overture. Banners had been draped overhead and flags*

waved at this brave group of seamen. *The captain
still felt uneasy as he scanned the sky in all
directions, and when he looked ahead he could
see that Bachmann was doing the same thing,
completely ignoring the jovial surroundings.*

*Sometime during the night as the men
were all billeting down, a scream and shattering
glass awoke all of them. As the men charged
into the darkened room, they became aware
that Bachmann's bed was empty. The large
front window of the room had been completely
smashed, with all but some pieces of the frame
barely left.*

*The captain staggered sheepishly through
the doorway and bowed his head. As soon as
he had heard the crash, even though he was
separated from Bachmann's room by a large
hallway, Holtz knew that the beast had returned
and taken the man.*

"Captain Holtz never saw action again during the
war, and became a recluse afterward. Horst Steiner told
Grandfather that the Captain always felt guilty about
the whole episode with the beast; although everyone
knew nothing could save the men. When Holtz revealed
his story to his superiors, high command thought that
he had taken leave off his senses and relieved him off

his duties. Later, when U-301 sailed again under a new command, she set off into the Atlantic and vanished without a trace," Thomas said.

"But what happened to the creature when it entered the submarine?" Dan asked. "Why did its skin start to peel off?"

"Grandfather said that someone must have blessed the boat, or held religious meetings in that area, because the submarine became like a church to the beast, blessed, a holy place, you know."

"Yeah, like hallowed ground. I understand," Dan nodded as the big Indian spoke on.

"Had the Captain closed the outer hatch and kept the submarine submerged, the beast would probably have been destroyed. Grandfather said this would have been so. This unknown power that attacked the creature would have been much too strong for it, but the price might been the death of the crew."

"What about the chanting? The Great Sundance that was written about in Sarah's letter?" Dan asked.

Thomas stared at the floor for a moment, and Dan felt that the big Indian was uncomfortable with the question.

"This information was given to Otis, and was only for Otis. It is a private thing. The Great Sundance is about self-sacrifice, and this is exactly what Otis had to do. Grandfather knew Otis would have to die in order to save his wife's life, and he felt he had sent the big fella to his death."

Thomas opened a side drawer and took out a thin necklace with a small carved totem on the end.

"This belonged to Grandfather, and for many years, it has lain in that drawer. Please take it! It will help to ward off the evil forces that occupy this world. Wear it at all times as I do," he said. He pulled an identical one out from under his shirt for Dan to see.

Dan put the necklace in place and thanked Thomas.

"Now I have to go to Ireland," he said.

# CHAPTER 12

Francis Flannagan had been lonely as a child. James Flannagan's family had disowned Rose when they found out about her affair with Frank Quinn, the Priest. Even Rose's own family had snubbed her and this child she had named after him. But Rose's vow to love and cherish the child faded under the burden of raising her alone.

Francis was a strong child, and she grew to be an even stronger woman. She had never known what a stable home was like. She had also known since she was young girl that she was the product of an illicit affair between her mother and the village priest.

No details of her parents' sins had been spared her. Other children had cruelly taunted her about it endless times over the years. She also knew that her mother's husband, James, had shot and killed the priest. The bullies had tried their worst with her, but Francis had always kept her dignity. She only cried when no one could see her.

As Francis grew up, she tried to understand why she was never allowed to visit with her grandparents, aunts and uncles like the other children in school. There was no one in her family, except her mother. She hated hearing about all the presents, compliments, and hugs the others received. Francis wasn't even allowed to keep a pet, not so much as a hamster.

Her mother, although twisted and bitter about life, kept the house spotless, and most of the time Francis was also kept busy cleaning. Even when the place didn't need cleaning, there would be Francis, mopping away...

The only real comfort Francis had was an old teddy bear that someone had left in the back garden for her. She had kept the teddy bear hidden from her mother for years and had formed a bond with the ragged bear she named "Mr Cliff." She had played and talked to the bear, and used a funny voice when it was his turn to speak. Yes, Mr Cliff was her dearest friend.

One day, when she was eleven years old, and playing with the bear, her mother burst in on her.

"Who is in here with you?" Rose thundered.

"No-one mother, I'm alone."

"Don't you bloody lie to me, girl, I heard voices."

"No, mother, it was only me, playing."

Listening from the hall, Rose had heard two distinctly different voices. One voice was unmistakably that of Francis, but the other was a much deeper voice, a rasping, pulsating sort of voice. She searched through the small wardrobe and under the bed. Francis had no chance to hide the bear properly, and so she had simply stuffed it under her blanket.

Rose was about to walk out of the room, when she turned and stared at the bed.

"No mother," Francis shouted. But she was too late.

Rose had pulled the bedclothes back.

"What the hell is this?" she asked, as she stared at the little scraggly bear.

"It's Mr Cliff, my best friend. Please don't take him," Francis begged.

Mr Cliff lay motionless, staring up.

"Run, Mr Cliff, run," Francis shouted at the bear, as if it could hear her.

Yet, the bear stayed still.

"Talking to bloody stuffed toys now are you," her mother scolded. "Its no wonder your schoolwork is the lowest in the class. Well I'll soon put a bloody stop to that.

Rose grabbed the bear. Francis lunged forward and managed to get a gip on Mr Cliff, but her mother tugged hard, and his leg tore off in her hand.

"Nooo…" Francis screamed at her mother, but Rose and the bear had gone. Francis fell back onto the bed and cried. She clutched the little furry leg, and cried herself to sleep once again.

The dream she had that night didn't seem like a dream, but somehow felt real.

*Francis listened to her mother singing. Somehow she knew this was a dream, because her mother just didn't sing.*

*Maybe before the bad things had happened her mother had sang, Francis thought.*

*Then the singing stopped and her mother's bedroom light turned off. The room was engulfed in almost in total darkness, except for a small ray of moonlight that lit up a far corner. Then Francis heard a voice.*

*'Come on, Francis,' the voice said, 'Come here.' It was Mr Cliff's voice.*

*He's come back to me, she thought, smiling. But she couldn't see him in the room, and his voice was faint.*

*'Where are you?' Francis whispered, afraid of her mother hearing her.*

*'I'm out here,' came the reply. 'Hurry up, girl!'*

*Francis pushed her feet from the bed and tiptoed to the door.*

*'Yes, come on,' Mr Cliff said.*

*Francis silently opened the bedroom door, and slipped out onto the landing. A funny smell invaded her nostrils. Flowers, it was flowers.*

*If I'm dreaming, how come I can smell flowers? Francis thought.*

*A waft of cold air blew around her naked legs. Then a bolt of lightning lit up the landing, followed by the biggest crash of thunder she had ever heard. She had lain in bed through many thunderstorms before, but she always had Mr Cliff to comfort her.*

*She just couldn't see him in the darkness. Then, when another flash of lightning appeared, she decided to run and hop back into her bed, where she would feel safer.*

*'C'mon Francis, in here' the voice sounded again.*

*It was louder this time and somewhere near.*

'*Where are you Mr Cliff?*' Then Francis thought she heard her mother's voice.

'*Heeelp, he is kil…*' the voice pleaded, before trailing off.

*Francis flung her mother's bedroom door opened, just as another flash went off. She was very frightened, but she bravely stepped toward her mother's bed. Another lightning bolt lit the room. At first she could only see her mother's face. It was purple, and her eyes bulged. She clutched at her throat. Something was choking her. It looked like a cat. No not a cat, smaller. It was…*

'*Die you, fucker,*' the voice shouted. '*Die!*'

'*Mr Cliff, no,*' Francis screamed. But Mr Cliff wasn't for listening. Mr Cliff was choking her mother to death.

'*Leave her alone!*' she shouted at the one legged bear. '*Leave my mother alone.*'

*Francis grabbed Mr Cliff and pulled with all her might as her mother's eyes bulged wider, and her face went darker.*

'*I hate you, leave her alone, you little bastard.*'

*Mr Cliff released Rose, and as he did, his head tore off in Francis's small hands. He turned his eyes toward her.*

'*It was all for you. I loved you,*' he said. *Then his blue eyes turned white, and he remained silent and still.*

*Francis had also loved Mr Cliff, but she just couldn't let him do this to her mother.*

*Her mother gurgled, and Francis thumped her chest. Suddenly she coughed violently and wheezed deeply as the colour returned to her cheeks. She would live.*

*Then everything went dark, and the dream suddenly ended.*

Someone was shaking her awake. When Francis opened her eyes there were some people around her bed—two policemen and a police woman. Another plain clothes woman sat clutching a board, and a priest stared down at her. Francis immediately felt pain in her arms, and when she looked down at them they were covered in cuts and bruises. A burning sensation ran up and down them.

"What happened to me?" Francis asked.

The smiling policewoman spoke to her first. "Come and get dressed child, and we will take you to the station. We can talk there."

The plain clothes woman kept asking her for her personal details, which she quickly wrote down.

"Why are you asking me all of these questions? Where's my mother?" Francis pleaded.

The stern-faced policeman spoke up rather sternly. "Your mother has been taken to hospital because of your serious assault on her. You almost killed her."

"No, I never touched her. Why don't you ask her? She'll tell you I didn't."

"Your mother has already implicated you in the assault."

The friendly policewoman spoke again, "If you didn't do it child, then who did?"

Francis paused for a moment, afraid. But she would tell them the truth, whatever the consequences.

"Mr Cliff done it," Francis sobbed, knowing that she was betraying her only, and dearest friend.

"Where does this Mr Cliff live, child?" the policewoman asked.

"He lives here," she answered. "He's in the next room, mother's room. But please don't take him away; it was mother who hurt him first!"

The policemen ran into the other room, while Francis followed closely behind.

"Where is he?" he said.

Francis pointed to the floor. "There he is. My teddy," she sobbed. "Mr Cliff."

The friendly policewoman was no longer friendly now after this, and she roughly held on to Francis's wrist.

"You're coming with us," she ordered.

"Tell them you done it, Mr Cliff," Francis shouted. "Oh please, tell them!"

But the little bears head remained still and silent.

They all left the house, and the rooms were now in darkness. The little bear's head lay where it had fallen, and its eyes partly lit up.

"I loved you, Francis," it whispered. "I loved you."

After this incident, Francis was put into different care homes. It was one year later to the day of the attack, when Francis was informed of her mother's death, but she was spared the details. They simply told that her mother had drowned in the bath-tub. Francis didn't really take it too badly, because Rose had never even come to visit her, or sent her a card or present.

But Francis knew who had done the killing. It was Mr Cliff, and he would have his revenge.

Francis wished her father was still alive. She felt the priest would have loved her deeply and cared for her. Frank Quinn would not have given in to people's prejudices, but he was dead, and she would had to soldier on alone.

Francis had married when she turned twenty, but eight years later she would be back on her own again. Martin Rankin was an even worse bully to her than the kids at school or her mother had been put together. He had beaten and abused her, and constantly left her without housekeeping money. Up to this point in her life, Francis had always believed and accepted that God was punishing her for the sins of her parents. She felt it was always going to be this way for her, but something was about to change in her unsettled life.

Francis knew all about the creature that people had said lurked in the woods, because Francis had seen it first hand.

*Martin Rankin, her husband had come home one night in a sweat, rambling and incoherent, and had taken to his bed.*

*It was three full days later when he finally pulled himself together. He had come downstairs fully dressed and ordered Francis to make him a meal.*

*He told Francis that he had seen a demon in the forest, three nights previously, when taking a short cut home from the pub. It had caressed his face, before floating off.*

*Francis knew that there was no short cut home through the forest. He had been in the there with Fiona Martin. She had heard about the carrying on between her husband and Fiona, but she didn't care anymore. She had no feelings left for him, not since he had bad-mouthed her and called her a bloody priest's cast off. He could have chased and slept with every other woman in the village after that, for all she cared.*

*Later that night, after he came in drunk again from the pub, she felt him slip into her bed. He pulled at her nightgown, kissing at her neck. The smell of drink from his drooling lips sickened her. It had been a long time since she had slept with him, and she didn't miss it at all.. Francis craved a man's love, a real true love. Just not with Martin Rankin. And even the thought of being with him, left her feeling nauseated.*

*'What's wrong, doesn't Fiona want you tonight?' Francis asked.*

*'Wh-whooose bl-bloody Fin-iona?' Rankin slurred, pretending he'd never heard of her.*

*Francis pushed him forcefully away and he fell awkwardly in a heap. She leapt from the bed, running and stumbling bare-footed downstairs and out into the back garden. There would be another beating coming, she knew, and she almost threw up at the thought of it. A distant thunderclap broke the night's silence, and an unexpected squall of rain blew into her face.*

*Francis began to cry and leaned heavily against the old rusted gate, ignoring the rain that was penetrating her hair and night-clothes. She could hear Rankin inside the house, searching and cursing her.*

*Francis decided then and there that she had had enough. She would face up to him. Wait for him to come out. And this time it would be different. This time she would fight back against him. Tonight she would finally show Martin Rankin that he had beaten her for the last time. She picked up a large stone from the garden floor and waited.*

*The booming thunder was drawing ever nearer now. The loud crash sounded as though it was directly overhead, as the house and garden lit up. Francis would not give Martin a chance. As soon as he came through the door she would hit him with all her might, and she held the heavy stone above her head.*

*KRRRAAASH, the overhead thunder roared.*

*Francis felt a movement beside her. A very slow movement, high to her right, somewhere in the dark. Almost near enough to touch her. Then, she felt a presence loom large beside her*

145

*and she dropped the stone. Francis couldn't see it, but she instinctively knew it was there.*

*As the sky lit up again she slowly lifted her head and looked through the swirling rain. Francis gasped and choked at the frightening, hooded figure that hovered just a few feet away. Its head jerked unnaturally, as it ignored her and looked toward the house. It held something in its hand, something small. It was a teddy bear's head, it was Mr Cliff.*

*Francis fell back and clutched the gate. It was Mr Cliff who had brought the demon to her husband in the forest. Mr Cliff had saved her.*

*The monk-like figure made no movement toward her. It simply turned its head to one side and gently sniffed at the air. The creature slowly held out its large, gnarled hand and pointed a long finger toward the house. As a lightning bolt lit the sky again, Francis stepped back in awe.*

*In the background she could hear Martin rummaging around inside the house. The creature had heard him, too, and it jerked forward in a very unnatural movement, as it focused on the house. Francis knew that this creature and Mr Cliff were not there to harm her. She became less frightened, and decided to confront the creature.*

*'Have you come for Martin?' she asked matter of factually.*

*The creature hissed loudly at her as it quickly jerked its head to one side, and Mr Cliff said nothing.*

*Francis nodded at the beast, almost bowing, and slowly backed away.* "Wait!" *she said, and darted back inside the house.*

'So there you are, you fucking whore,' the half naked man spat. 'Next time you walk away from me like that, I'll bloody kill you, do you hear me?'

*She pulled away from him as he screamed into her face, his eyes ablaze with hate.*

'There's someone out back to see you, Martin,' she said and pointed toward the back garden.

'Out back. What do you mean out back?' he slurred, suspicious of her. 'Who the bloody hell is it?'

'Its Fiona, she wants to speak to you. She's waiting for you in the garden.'

'I'm warning you, you bloody better not be lying to me,' Martin raged, as he staggered out into the cold night.

'There's no one here,' she heard him shout

'Yes, there is,' Francis lied. 'She's waiting down by the tree.'

'There's no one fu...'

*When Francis stepped back out into the garden, Martin was no longer there. She looked up into the sky, but could see nothing. The toy bear's head lay on the ground, unmoving. Francis hurriedly picked up Mr Cliff and simply walked back into the house. She gently closed the door, and as the thunderstorm moved on, she hugged the little bear's head tightly. They would never be separated again.*

Francis had reported her husband missing, as any dutiful wife should, and the police had assumed that Martin had simply run off. The police already knew just what a loose cannon of a man Martin Rankin was, and were aware his affairs with various women in the village.

Fiona had threatened and accused Francis of murdering Martin. She caused a scene in the street on more than one occasion, and had also called Francis a witch.

Francis had not been involved with any man since. She had passed the exams, and gone to the police Academy, and was now the only female police officer in Cappawhite. Although very professional in her job, Francis got great pleasure when a drunken Fiona was arrested for shoplifting. Francis had the pleasure of fingerprinting and locking her in a cell overnight. The downside was, even when sober, Fiona failed to recognise her the next day. *This is what the drink has done to her,* Francis thought, at the time.

Francis had known Tully for a long time, and had dealt with him many times in his capacity as gamekeeper. Although she often felt drawn to the handsome man, she had always kept her feelings for the married man in check. Tully had no idea that Francis felt anything more for him than simple friendship.

Tully was sipping at a cup of tea and staring at the floor when Francis entered the room.

"Hello, Tully. How are you?" she smiled, surprised, but happy to see him. If Tully had looked into her eyes at that moment, they would have betrayed her true feelings for him.

But, Tully sat and stared straight ahead.

Francis knelt down beside him and lovingly held his hand. In response, Tully gently squeezed hers.

"Things haven't been so good for me lately, Fra," he answered. Tully was the only one who called her that, but she didn't mind. It was a personal thing. "What about you, Fra, have you been alright?"

"If you mean, am I still on my own? Then yes, I am. Once bitten, you know."

Tully knew only too well. He had gone to school with the bullying Martin Rankin, and despised him. He had also been the only boy in the school who had stood up to him. The fight in the playground with Rankin had left Tully bruised and battered, but he had won the fight. In any event, Tully felt it was a lucky punch and he knew he might not be so lucky next time.

When he first heard about Francis marrying Rankin, he had prayed for her. Tully could never understand just what qualities Francis had seen in the man, but he supposed that in this case love really was blind. Then Rankin had disappeared, and even Tully suspected foul play on her part. But even if Rankin's body had been found with ten daggers sticking from it, and a confession from Francis pinned to his chest, Tully believed the police would have been reluctant to prosecute. This was because Francis was so well liked by anyone she met.

Tully would not look badly on Fra either, because he would gladly have killed the bastard himself, given a chance. Many times though, he wondered just how she had disposed of his body.

"I'm sorry about you and Madge," Francis said.

"Please, Fra, I don't wish to talk about it. Let's just say, it's over," he groaned.

Francis caressed his face before walking from the room, and Tully felt puzzled at her behaviour.

"Pretty girl, and a police woman, too," Dan exclaimed, as he passed her in the doorway.

Tully didn't answer, but continued to stare solemnly at the cup.

It just never occurred to Tully that a girl as beautiful as Francis would have any interest in him. Some years earlier, Tully had taken a group of kids from the school out camping in the forest. There were three teachers and forty children in the group.

Francis had volunteered to help when the fourth teacher had a family emergency, and couldn't go on the trip. Tully's aim was to teach the children basic survival skills over the three-day camp, and to make sure they all had some fun. He also hoped that the kids would bond with one another, and also learn how to work together as a team.

On the first night, the only male teacher, Mr Harding, had gotten himself drunk. Earlier in the day he had also made untoward advances toward Francis. She had turned him down, and he stormed off in a huff, returning later that night more inebriated than he had been before. Harding tried to force his way into Francis's tent, and he was loudly abusing her when Tully got there.

Nearly all of the children had been awakened the commotion, and some were crying. The other female teachers had tried to persuade Harding to return to his tent, but they were met with another barrage of his abuse.

Tully tried to talk to him, but it was clear to everyone that Harding just wasn't going to listen. Tully pushed him into Francis's tent which was empty, and zipped the door behind him. There was a thud, and one minute later Tully emerged with three sleeping bags in his arms.

"Mr Harding has agreed to sleep it off until morning," he said. "You ladies will have to share my tent, and I'll take his."

The next day Mr Harding emerged from the tent nursing a first rate headache and holding his aching jaw. Tully ordered him to leave, and after some grovelling apologies, he marched off, red-faced.

"Tully is a natural born leader. And quite handsome as well," Francis said, right in front of everyone. As she thanked him, she also kissed his cheek.

Tully had shown no interest then. He had simply nodded and walked off with a half-smile.

# CHAPTER 13

It was a day later when Dan arrived in Ireland, tired and dishevelled, but anxious to carry out his job and get to the bottom of the strange happenings in Cappawhite.

The morning was clear and dry, and Donald O'Shea was there to greet him at the airport. The two men shook hands as though they were old friends. The journey back to Cappawhite was filled with the explanation of every detail the old policeman could remember about the beast. Donald described the horrible ending in the hospital theatre where Otis bravely forfeited his life trying to save Sarah.

Dan felt immediately at ease with the friendly officer, and had listened intently to his account of the events with great interest. This wasn't some drunken village idiot telling him stories and gossip, but a highly respected senior policeman, who had witnessed these events first hand.

Yet, Dan was unsure how to take this all in. His training and normal sense of logic told him this was serious bullshit, but all the brutal, mysterious deaths, and eye-witness accounts involved with the sightings couldn't be denied. Dan knew that he would best serve this story by keeping an open and honest mind.

As they pulled up outside the station in Cappawhite, Sergeant Blair McCann was standing there, waiting to greet them. Dan noticed a man on the other side of the street stare wildly at him.

The man had something in his hand that he seemed to be hiding behind his legs.

*A baseball bat perhaps,* Dan thought, and he stopped to look back.

"Oh, don't worry about him," Sergeant McCann said, realising that Dan found the man staring at him rather intimidating. "That's only Griff. He likes to keep the village tidy, and is always intensely interested in any strangers that come to visit. He's harmless though!"

The stick that Dan thought was a baseball bat was actually a grab arm for lifting rubbish. He felt foolish.

Go on about your business, Griff," the sergeant shouted across to the man.

Suddenly Griff looked away and began to lift pieces of rubbish from the roadside.

"Yeah," Blair went on. "Griff has the mental age of an eight year old, but he keeps the village spotless. Does it for free as well, and everyone in the village donates some money for him every week."

As Dan stared at Griff, the child-like man glanced back at him, and smiled.

As they entered the small station in Cappawhite, Dan was surprised at the amount of activity that was going on inside. There were high-ranking police officers there as well as high-ranking military personnel everywhere, and Dan was quite impressed.

"I see you guys are leaving no stone unturned," he said.

Over in the corner, a captain was very loudly berating a young corporal. He screamed at the red faced youth," Look at the state of your damn tunic. Do you think you're in the bloody Black-N-Tans?"

"We must evacuate the town, and all areas within a twenty mile radius," Donald said to one of the officers, ignoring Dan. "We can use the same excuse as last time, dangerous chemical spillage. Hughes, please get on to it right away and make sure it's posted to the wire as well."

"Yes, Sir. Right away, Sir," the officer replied before quickly marching away.

That done, Donald turned to Dan, again giving him his full attention. He placed his hand onto Dan's shoulder, and he gently guided him out into the corridor.

"C'mon, Dan, I would like you to meet Tully. He has witnessed this creature personally." he said, leading Dan into another room.

Tully was sitting trancelike at the table, while a small police sergeant was vigorously questioning him in a very intimidating manner. The sergeant accused Tully of assault.

"Sergeant McGrath, what's going on here?" Donald asked.

"This man assaulted someone over at the Ross Inn in the early hours of this morning, Sir. Gave him a right good going over he did, and I'm questioning him about it."

Donald roughly pulled the small sergeant back across the room, and snapped at him. "There is something out there in the forest, killing our bloody people, and we need this man, Tully, to help us find and destroy it. Do you understand me? Now I don't care if he assaulted his Holiness the Pope himself. I don't want him arrested, questioned, charged, slapped on the wrist, or even spoken to harshly. Am I making this quite clear to you?"

"Yes sir, but he has committed an offence," the irate sergeant answered.

Donald wrenched the charge sheet from the stunned sergeant's hands and tore it in two. He simply said two words. "No charges!"

The sergeant walked quickly from the room, his face like thunder, but Tully didn't seem to notice, or care for that matter. He merely sat there and continued to stare into space.

Donald introduced Dan to Sergeant Blair McCann, and then, Tully. The three men sat down, joining Tully at the large table.

"Tully, my boy, you are going to have to snap the hell out of the mood you're in, if you're to be of any use to us at all. You are going to keep your promise to help, aren't you?" Donald stated to him. His tone was forceful, almost demanding a response.

Tully sat, tearful in his chair as the others stared at him. Then he raised his head and looked at each man, before speaking.

"Yes, I will help. I want to—I need to," he whispered.

Dan left the room and got himself a cold coke, and wandered back into the room as Donald was walking out.

"What's the story with that guy, Tully?" Dan asked.

"He's having woman problems. His wife left him some months ago and the poor man just cannot deal with it."

Dan walked over and once again sat at the table. He noisily squeezed at his coke tin with his finger and thumb. *Click-click-click, click-click-click,* it went.

Tully continued staring into space, ignoring Dan. Then he raised an eyebrow at the aggravating man in front of him.

"Are you alright there, friend?" Dan asked Tully. He was enjoying this, and he watched as the man began to eyeball him wildly.

Yet Tully remained motionless and silent. Dan continued to play with the tin. *Click-click, click-click, click-click-click.* Then Dan suddenly stopped and lobbed the tin into a wastebasket that sat all the way across the room.

"You know, you remind me of my wife. Her name is Beatrice," Dan went on.

Tully raised his head higher and squinted his eyes toward Dan in a threatening manner.

"Yeah, well how do you figure that out?" Tully croaked, feeling a bit undignified at where the Yank was going with this, and how he was talking to him.

"Well, I'm sorry if I sound rude, pal, but you're bottling something up here. My wife does the same thing. It isn't healthy."

"Well, maybe Beatrice has a bloody reason to bottle it up—seeing as she's married to you," Tully spat.

"There's no need for you to get all riled up and personal there friend. I'm only saying, maybe you should talk to someone," Dan answered.

"Oh, I didn't know we had a fucking psychiatrist on board," Tully said loudly. "Why you don't even know me. Who the bloody hell are you to question me about my life?"

"Well I'm sorry if I offended you, and of course, your right. It's none of my damn business," Dan answered sheepishly as he put his feet on the table, hands behind his head. "All I know is, I don't bottle it up. I try to get over it, and then get on with it."

No one spoke for some time again, until Dan broke the silence. He told Tully about his own woman troubles, explained about how his wife had only just left him.

Tully had mellowed somewhat. *Here's a man with as many problems as I have, probably more,* he thought. *But this fella is behaving the way a man should. Getting over it, and getting on with it. During these sorts of circumstances, it's the only dignity a man's got left!*

"Is there no chance for you and your wife then?" Tully asked.

"Nope!" Dan replied. "And it's happened to plenty of men before we came along. Better men than us Tully. So we will just have to live with it and move forward. Right now, we need to help these policemen with this situation. Our problems will just have to wait until later."

Tully thought about his father for a moment. That was the kind of thing his father would have said before the fire.

"You are damn right, Yank. I'll go along with that," Tully said. He leaned across the table and shook Dan by the hand.

"Now where can I get some cigarettes? I know, damn disgusting habit, but every man has at least one," Dan said.

Donald, who had returned to the room, pointed to the door.

"At the shop…sorry, I mean store. It's just around the corner," Donald said.

"I know what a shop is," Dan laughed, as he got up from the table.

Dan walked out of the police station and onto the street. A fresh breeze blew into his face and the unfamiliar smell of freshly laid manure from one of the neighbouring farms wafted into his nostrils.

*So this is Ireland*, he thought, as he breathed in deeply, filling his lungs. The smell was almost appealing.

Tully suddenly appeared behind him.

"Hi again," Dan said, slightly startled.

"I needed some fresh air," Tully answered, as he walked alongside Dan. "Mind if I accompany you?"

"Not at all, you are welcome to come along, Tully."

Then Dan raised his arm, and patted Tully on the back. Tully smiled. Dan already thought he noticed a change in the man.

"So you have seen the creature then?" Dan asked.

"Yes, and I hope never to see it again."

"What was it like?" Dan probed.

"Well, it's a big bloody thing, I'll tell you that. Frightening, and with awesome power. And it can fly!" Tully added, and started to tear up. "It killed all of those young soldiers. It just tore them limb from…"

"It's alright, Tully. We can talk about this some other time, when you are feeling up to it," Dan said softly.

As they turned the corner, Dan saw Griff on the other side off the road. Only this time he was not alone. There were three youths circling around the gentle man, menacing him. Griff stood helpless as a foetus, pressed against the wall.

"Give us some money, or we'll fucking kill you, Griff," they heard one of the youths say.

"Hey, assholes," Dan shouted. "Leave him alone."

The boys turned around to see who dared to confront them. Recognizing Tully and his reputation, the boys thought the better for it, and ran off.

"You alright there, Griff?" Dan asked, as the frightened Griff backed away slightly.

"Griff don't have no money," he droned, as a small bit of spittle ran from the corner of his mouth.

"Well Griff, you're alright now. You just give old Dan or Tully here a shout if those assholes annoy you again. All right?" Dan said, He narrowed his eyes, and stared at the trio of boys, who were now just dots fading into the distance.

Griff nodded nervously, before slowly sauntering down the street. He continued to instinctively pick up the litter and transfer it to a plastic trash bag.

As Dan and Tully crossed the road, an old man stopped them and shook their hand, "Seen what you fella's did there. It's about time someone stood up to that rabble. They just won't leave that poor man alone."

"Who are they?" Dan asked.

"Well, the ring leader is Fred Kelly, but I don't know the other two. That Kelly though—he's a bad egg. Damn well likely to kill someone someday, just wait and see," the old man said as he slowly turned away. He walked on slowly down the street, and continued to mutter to himself.

They finally reached the store, and Dan purchased the cigarettes. The two men then walked slowly back to the station, the incident already forgotten.

Tully continued to talk about the beast that was lurking in the forest, and fully explained to Dan about what he had seen. He spoke once more about the soldiers it had killed. Only this time he wasn't sobbing. Then he added the grim details of Lamont's Mine.

"I think its staying in there during the day," Tully said.

"Are you sure about that?" Dan asked.

"Sure as I am about anything."

Dan paused for a moment and stared at Tully.

"If your right about that mine, then I just might know how to kill that thing," Dan answered. "Come on, I want to share some ideas with you and the officers.

Soon Dan had related the story to the other three men about Thomas Lapahie's tale of the German submarine, and how the creature almost died inside the blessed vessel.

"So you are saying, that if we can trap this thing on hallowed ground, then we can kill it?" Donald asked.

"Yes, I believe we can. But we'll only hold it there and tire it. We won't do the actual killing—another, greater power will do that for us," Dan answered.

"But how do we get this creature to come to somewhere like that, and you're talking about a church, right?" Blair asked.

"We don't," Dan said excitedly.

All the men looked at him with puzzled expressions.

"And I'm not talking about a church either. I'm talking about Lamont's Mine."

Now the two policemen looked even more confused. Tully pounded Dan on the back and stood up.

"Brilliant! Good God, that's it!" Tully exclaimed.

"Tully and I believe that the creature is hiding out in Lamont's Mine during the daylight hours. If we go in there at night, with a priest, while the creature is roaming the forest, then we can have the place blessed. When it returns, we simply block the entrance. Then God can sort it out from there."

"How do you know it stays in Lamont's Mine? Donald asked.

"Believe me, it's in the mine. I've seen it there," Tully said.

From that moment on, everything went into over-drive. Dan found himself bundled into a car with the other three men.

"Where the hell are we going?" Dan enquired.

"To Tipperary, to see Father Blake, the most knowledgeable priest in Ireland," Blair answered. "If he can't help us, then no one else can."

Over an hour later, they were finally able to see Father Blake. It took another full hour to explain the entire story to him, but after listening to the men, the priest seemed unmoved.

"First of all, to bless this mine you speak of, I would need permission from the highest authority, Rome. Landowners would need to be consulted, and newspapers informed. It can take months before the church sanctions such a thing," Father Blake said. "It's not like the old days when a priest just made these sorts of decisions at will."

"We don't have months Father; we probably don't even have days. The towns and farms all around for a twenty mile radius are being evacuated tomorrow, including this one, and we are unsure how this creature will react once the area becomes deserted," Donald said.

"I'm sorry," said the old priest. "There's nothing I can do."

"Well you should bloody do something," said Tully, angrily. "I saw what this abomination can do, and if it's not stopped—then many more innocent people are going to die. Do you want that on your conscience?"

Donald turned away, and stared across the pews, at the ornamental statuettes and the cross with Jesus staring back toward him. He felt sick to the pit of his stomach with the realisation that they were getting nowhere fast.

"C'mon, I know where we can get some help. Not everybody is so scared of what the higher-ups think," said Tully,.

Donald turned pleadingly to the old priest. Father Blake stared hard at the floor, seemingly unconcerned, yet unable to meet anyone's eyes.

"Will you not see reason, father?" Donald asked one more time.

Father Blake did not answer, but simply lowered his head even more. Donald stared at him, unable to hide his feelings of contempt for this man.

"I didn't expect you to be so useless or the Church to be so powerless," he said, before sauntering out through the door, followed closely by the other three men.

Once inside the car, Tully spoke first. "Drive out toward the village of Doon, to St Patrick's church," he ordered.

The other two police officers looked at each other.

"But that's a Protestant church?" said Sergeant McCann, confused.

"Aye, and my uncle, McLeay, is the minister there.

There was a moment's awkward silence, before Tully spoke again.

"Oh, I see," Tully said laughing. "So you didn't know I was a Protestant!"

"I couldn't care less if you are a damn Buddhist," exclaimed Donald. "If you can get this bloody cave blessed, then I'll be happy to settle for that."

"Um, it's a mine," Tully advised.

"Cave or mine, either way it's just a bloody big hole in the ground," Donald said.

"Let's just go get the minister," Dan said.

Soon the men had reached the outskirts of Doon, and Donald re-checked his watch.

"We'll have to hurry," he said. "It will be dark in an hour, and we don't want to be driving these roads at night. Not when that demon's in the woods.

Blair swung the car heavily into the bends, as Donald, Dan and Tully scanned the trees on either side.

Then they had arrived, and a surprised Rev McLeay invited them into a side room. Donald did most of the talking, occasionally backed up by the other men, and the minister listened intently.

"I always knew there was something out there in those woods," he said. "I've heard all sorts of stories. This is a very dangerous situation we have here. If this plan of yours fails to work, then you may actually drive the abomination into other towns. It may seek some sort of retribution, and kill everyone it can get to."

"At the moment, it's doing plenty of that already," Donald said.

"It certainly is," Constable McCann added, backing up his superior.

"Damn right," Dan whispered in affirmation.

The old minister fiddled with an old worn domino and moved it around his fingers like a magician. Back and forward he went with it, seemingly unaware of what he was doing, as he stared ahead.

Tully finally broke the silence. "Will you help us then, uncle?" he asked.

After a brief pause, the minister pushed the domino into his pocket and looked at the men solemnly over the rim of his glasses.

"Yes Tully, I will."

"We will have to make some arrangements first though," Donald said.

Cameras would have to be positioned high in the trees. They would have to be placed so they could see in all directions, within about a quarter of a mile from the mine. This safety perimeter had to be observed, lest the beast return unexpectedly and kill them all before they had begun.

Tomorrow they would come and pick up Rev McLeay. They would arrive sometime after noon. Donald thanked Rev McLeay, and shook his hand, before they all sped off, back toward Cappawhite.

For the first time Donald thought they had a real chance to end this thing for good. If Tully was right about the mine, it was the answer to their prayers. They would finally rid themselves of the beast. No one outside of their circle need ever know what they had done, but they would rid the world of a foul monster. This knowledge would be reward enough for them.

Donald also knew that there might be more than one of these creatures roaming the earth, only God knew how many. But if one of them could be killed, then so could the rest.

Daylight was beginning to fade now, and the men felt relieved as they entered Cappawhite.

# CHAPTER 14

Madge left the Ross Inn as the men pulled in at the station. Tully spotted her familiar figure in the distance, walking out toward the edge of town. She wasn't carrying any luggage or handbag, and Tully thought this unusual.

"Excuse me, there's something I have to tend to" he said, quickly leaving the car to run after her.

Tully was unsure of what he was going to say to Madge, or how she would react to him. Regardless of what may happen, he could never go back to her. He would never be able to forgive her for this act of betrayal. He still had strong feelings for her though, and he would have to stop her from going out this night and leaving the village, before she did something that could only be considered as suicidal.

"Hello, Madge! Where are you going?" he asked, and moved in quickly in front of her.

"H-Hello Tully," she choked. Red-eyed, she pushed him aside, and continued to walk on.

Tully dropped in beside her, and wondered just how he was going to stop the headstrong woman from leaving the village.

The other three men had exited the car now and they stared after them.

"Where the hell is he going?" Dan asked, as he looked up into the sky. Darkness had fallen, and stars glittered overhead. It was night already and they hadn't even noticed it coming on.

"We can't just let them walk out of town like that," Blair said. "We need Tully."

"Drive past them and don't let them leave the village. If they get as far as Ironmills Bridge, arrest them," Donald ordered.

"On what charge?" asked Blair, rather naively.

"Jaywalking, vagrancy—any damn charge. Just go!" Donald answered sharply.

Blair drove up the street, and slowly passed the couple, but they seemed unaware of him.

I'm sorry for the hurt I caused you, Tully," Madge said.

"Why, Madge, why did you do it?" he answered.

"You mean to say, you don't know Tully? You where never there for me, Tully," she cried. "I tried to talk to you many times, but you just wouldn't listen. You just weren't bloody there!"

"And he-he was bloody th-there for you, I suppose, huh?" Tully stuttered.

Madge bowed her head and remained silent as she continued to walk along. She knew about her new lover running off with the landlady's daughter. In fact, she had known in her heart all along what Gary Storey was like, but she had fallen in love with the two-timing serial cheat anyway. Now it was all over, and she just didn't want to go on anymore.

"We can't go any further. It's dangerous," Tully said as they neared the edge of the village.

"Please don't try to stop me," Madge answered as she wiped a tear away. "I'm going back to Tipperary to see my mother. Please leave me alone!"

"No, Madge, there's something lurking out there in the woods. You wouldn't get halfway to Tipperary."

Madge ignored him, gave a shrug of her shoulder's, and was about to walk on, when suddenly Sergeant McCann appeared from out of the darkness.

"I'm sorry, Madge," he said to the distraught woman. "I cannot let you go on. It's not safe. There's a chemical spill not far up the road."

"It's alright, Blair. I've told her the truth!" Tully stated.

"Jesus, Tully, you did what?"

"Leave me alone," Madge interrupted, and broke away from the two men. "You can't make me stay. I'm going t..."

"You are going back with us," Tully ordered. He stepped in front of her and pulled at her coat.

"Don't you order me about you bastard! Do you understand?" Madge said. "I don't love you anymore. I don't ever want to be with you again. I despise you, you fucking lame excuse for a man."

Tully put his hands to his head at her barrage of insults, and suddenly it was like he was listening to his mother's voice. This was just like the abusive name-calling his mother had spewed at his father. Tully felt transformed, almost like he was in the centre of the living room of his parent's house, and his hate-filled mother was yelling at him. Only this time, he was not a little boy. This time he was a stronger man than his father had ever been, he simply turned and walked away. Madge continued to berate him, but Tully just kept walking.

Tully heard Blair's voice cry out loudly, as the Madge ran past him, hurrying over Ironmills Bridge. Then he snapped back out of it.

"No, Madge, come back!" Blair yelled, as she moved quickly up the dark country road.

Tully sprinted across the bridge behind Madge into the darkness, and Blair continued to yell after her,.

When Tully caught up with her, he grabbed her arm tightly. Madge fought like a wildcat, clawing and punching at him. She gouged his face, and caused it to bleed badly. Just as she shook herself free, and was about to sprint off again, Tully punched her. Madge fell to the ground. Tully picked her up in his arms and carried her back over the bridge, and soon Madge was bundled into the car. They all headed back to the police station in Cappawhite.

"You're hurt," Blair said, as he looked at Tully's bloodied face.

"I'm fine, Blair," Tully answered. "You must say Madge struck you also. That way you can charge her with assaulting a policeman. Then she'll be locked in a cell for tonight, safe and out of harms way."

"Don't worry, Tully, I'll do that."

Tully placed a handkerchief to his bleeding cheek, and looked around to the semi-conscious woman in the back seat. He still cared for her, despite everything she had said and done. He had never struck Madge before, and he felt bad that it went this far. Yet, part of him was happy——she would be safe.

"You're a bloody tiger, Madge," Tully whispered as he wiped his face.

After being examined for injuries, Madge was arrested and placed in the only cell available at the small station. She had never been in trouble before, and the woman was frightened as she lay on the hard, stained mattress and cried.

The phone rang, and Donald picked it up. He shook his head as his superior, on the other end, instructed him about their next course of action.

"But Alan…" Donald said. He didn't get another word in before hanging up and lowering the phone back into the cradle.

Donald looked anxiously at all of them for a moment.

"There is to be no evacuation. They say it would cause mass panic. Apart from that, there seems to have been a leak about our situation. Now we're in a race against time. Can you imagine what will happen if this gets out to the media? It'll be a damn circus. People will come to Cappawhite in droves to get a look at the demon we're hiding here. It'll be a bloodbath on a scale that I can't even dare think about now. We have to put this matter to bed tomorrow, or there's no chance of ending it quietly. We have to get all the rest we can. We will start first thing in the morning."

Tully borrowed an old blanket, and decided to bed down on a sofa in the corridor. He could still hear Madge crying. The sound travelled lightly to his ears from a distant cell, somewhere in the building. He pulled a borrowed pillow over his head, and tried to block out the sound.

Donald unlocked a panelled door, at the bottom of the corridor. The inside of the room, although small, was tastefully decorated. It also had a shower and toilet en-suite. This room had been sat aside for the very purpose of housing a visiting official. Donald would be one of the very few to have actually used it. The single bed had a large bright duvet, and Donald lay on top of it without bothering to get undressed. For some time he lay in the semi darkness, thinking about his wife and son, before sleep overtook him.

Sergeant Blair McCann gave Dan a guest voucher for the Ross Inn, and bade him goodnight.

Blair had witnessed the creature at the hospital thirty-five years ago. But he had hidden his face from it as it wailed, hissed, and tore Otis apart. Even though he was just a frightened teenager then, his fear was as strong now as it had been then. The only difference now was that he didn't fear death as much. In his line of work he had seen enough of death to make peace with it. He simply feared the act of dying itself. If this creature was not destroyed and turned on them, then he might not get the peaceful death from old age that he wanted.

Dan made his way to the Ross Inn, but had trouble getting someone to wait on him. He could see three women in an office behind the check-in counter.

The door to the room was open. An older woman was crying, and apparently being comforted by two women in maid's uniforms.

"I want Vera," the woman sobbed.

One of the maids who had noticed Dan staring in at them through the open door, stood up, and slammed the door.

He stood waiting for over fifteen minutes before one of them finally came, got his information and gave him a room key.

When Dan entered his bedroom he was amazed at its size. Two king-sized beds would not have been out of place there, but instead, it had two small singles. Still, he was very tired from all his travelling, and it wasn't long before he was sleeping like a baby.

Later, there was a commotion in the corridor, and Dan suddenly found himself sitting upright in bed, wide-awake. He tiptoed naked from the bed, and peeped around the door to investigate.

The older woman who had been crying in the office hugged and kissed a dishevelled girl. The girl's clothes were torn, and her face looked as though it had been scratched by brambles.

"Vera," she sobbed. "Vera!"

The maids were again beside her, looking on as the girl cried, and sobbed out a story to the women about a demon—a demon that had accosted her in the forest. She related how it had trapped her in the car, taunted her by licking the windows, and then flew off. When she believed it was truly gone, she got out of the car and ran. She had hidden out all day, afraid to move. When it started to get dark, she realised she had to get home or risk being attacked by it again.

"You wretched girl! You shouldn't scare your mother like that," snapped one of the maids. "You shouldn't make up stories like that."

"But I'm not making it up," Vera sobbed. "I did see it. I swear!"

Dan pulled on a pair of boxer shorts, and a bathrobe, and stepped out into the hallway. "Excuse me," he said. "I'm sorry, but I couldn't help overhearing. Could I talk to you about this demon?"

"This young lady is going to bed," said the maid. "Just look at the state she's in."

"What do you know about it, Mr Winters?" the other maid asked politely.

"Enough to know that Vera's not lying," he said.

Dan asked to speak to the mother and daughter alone, and they agreed. Soon they were sitting in the Ross living room. In order to gain the girl's trust, Dan decided to tell them everything he knew——except their plan at Lamont's Mine.

"Your daughter was lucky, Mrs Ross, because this thing is merciless. It roams the forest at night, and kills on a whim. It's like a lost soul, and a very dangerous lost soul at that."

"Can it be killed, Mr Winters?" the mother asked.

"We believe it can, under the right conditions. We are working on the solution now—but God help us, if it doesn't work."

Dan was puzzled about the reason that Vera had been spared. Vera said that the creature had sped off in hot pursuit, apparently after someone else. This just did not seem to fit the pattern. Staring at the girl, he noticed that she kept her pulling at her necklace.

"Mind if I see what that is?" Dan motioned to her necklace, and reached across and gently took the small pendant into his hands. He then removed his own necklace from under his robe, and compared them side by side.

"Wow! They're almost identical," Dan said. The totems were very similar, except that Vera's was much smaller. He wasn't sure if this was the reason the girl had been spared. But perhaps the Lakota Sioux knew a lot more than some people gave them credit for, and he tucked his own little totem away. Thankful now that Thomas Lapahie had given it to him.

Dan smiled at the sobbing frightened girl, then excused himself for a moment. When he returned he had one arm behind his back. "I've got something for you Vera, but you must promise to look after it forever."

Vera half-smiled and nodded, and Dan showed her the little poodle. "Free to a good home," Dan said, as Vera gently took it from his hand.

Dan didn't even know why he had packed the poodle, and couldn't even remember putting it in his luggage. He didn't want any reminders of his wasted marriage around, and maybe Vera would appreciate it.

As Dan walked back to his room, he thought about Beatrice, and whispered a small prayer for her. He realised the danger he hade gotten himself into, and almost wished he hadn't come to Ireland. But this story was probably the biggest one he had ever worked on, probably the biggest of his life.

# CHAPTER 15

There were fifteen cameras fitted securely high in the trees, onto the stronger branches. They had all been situated about a quarter of a mile from the mine, scanning in all directions. The workmen were unaware of what was lurking in the dark mine, simply being told that the cameras were being put there to catch a killer, who was hiding in the forest. They finished their work in record time though, and Donald felt sure it was because of the rumours surrounding this evil place. Those rumours that had simply been that—having no substance or credence. Yet, even unproven the story had enough sting in the tale to put the fear of God into everyone in the village.

*Like all rumours, they grow like a cancer. Fast* and *furious!* Donald thought. *Unless, of course, there is proof to the contrary.*

Maybe this time they would get their proof, through the lens of a camera, and then the idle speculation would be over. The cameras were linked to the small station in Cappawhite, with ten monitors and two men watching them at all times, and all the information was being recorded. They were taking no chances.

Donald knew the risk they were taking, but there was no other choice. He felt quietly confident though, that the plan would succeed.

The old minister from Doon had been brought to Cappawhite that day. Rev McLeay had insisted on bringing a younger colleague with him; a frail, sickly young man, whose white clerical collar looked three times too big for him. Donald was angry at the addition, because he had wanted to keep as few people as possible in the loop.

"This is Rev George Collins, whose help in this matter will be very important to us. Between us, we can have the mine blessed in half the time. Reverent Collins has just returned from Africa, from his missionary work. No doubt his parishioners will miss him dearly, but his health was deteriorating and the decision was made to bring him home," Rev McLeay stated.

The men all shook hands and sat down to discuss the issue before them.

It was agreed that they should go to Lamont's Mine immediately after dark. As soon as they were sure the mine was empty, then the ministers could go in and begin the consecration. A large wooden cross would be brought to the mine and used to block the small entrance, once the creature had moved inside. The workmen had checked the cameras, which worked perfectly, but the large batteries had to be changed daily. The cameras had sound sensors, and night vision capabilities.

The stern-faced, small sergeant that Donald had chastised the night before entered the room and called Donald outside.

Donald excused himself and left, but was only gone about five minutes. When he returned, he nodded solemnly at them, "That was a call from HQ in Dublin. We've been given two days to sort this mess out and find the murderer, or we're being taken off the case."

"Yeah, murderer," Tully laughed. "If they only knew the bloody truth, the ruddy fools."

"Well I think we have the matter in hand, boys," said Donald as he turned to the ministers, "It's all down to you two fellows now."

"Are you alright there, Rev Collins?" Tully asked the young minister.

Collins, who was sweating profusely, had been ignoring the conversation.

"Rev Collins has a slight case of jungle fever," Rev McLeay exclaimed, gripping the young ministers arm. "But he'll be just fine, won't you George?"

The young minister smiled awkwardly.

The men sat around until darkness came, and then began to intently study the cameras. Only the swaying of the trees showed up on the small screens, and the men were beginning to feel they may have been mistaken about Lamont's mine. Then a shadow came over one of the monitors.

"What was that?" Dan asked.

"Play it back, play it back!" Donald urged.

Soon all eyes were on the one-second clip, which revealed nothing, except a darkening of the light over the fixed camera.

"That's it," said Tully. "Don't you see?" The damn thing has come over the top of the trees."

"We can't be sure about that, Tully," Donald said, as he looked across to the ministers. "It was only a shadow and we have these men's safety to consider here above all else!"

"Yes, we can be sure! I saw it floating alongside the top of the trees twice before. This is where it travels, high in the branches. The shadow on the monitor must be the beast, going out into the forest. We may not get another damn chance at this."

"We cannot just take that chance Tully, we must be certain about this," Donald exclaimed.

"Well we can't just sit here and do nothing," Tully protested.

"Listen, why don't we all go over there and see for ourselves," Rev McLeay stated calmly, as he tried to remove some of the tension from the air.

"What do you think Dan?" Donald asked.

"I think Tully's right," Dan answered.

"All right," said Donald with an air of authority, "we'll go, but with as few men as possible. I won't have needless deaths on my conscience. Tully, the two clerics, and I will go. You stay here, Blair, in charge of the radio," he said, pointing at the sergeant. "And Dan can help with the monitoring."

Dan really wanted to accompany the men, but he bit his tongue and said nothing. He was just grateful that he had been allowed to participate at all.

The four men left the police station, and Dan couldn't help but notice that the younger minister was almost in a trance-like state. He watched him walk zombie-like, out through the door.

They had been gone a half-hour when Dan pulled out his cigarettes, but the box was almost empty. He hadn't any recollection of having smoked so many, and he was angry at himself. He needed a cigarette now though, badly, and he excused himself. He made his way around the corner to the store. The shop lights were on, but the large shutter was pulled down and locked.

"Damn!" Dan said, as he turned to walk back to the station. Then he heard a faint sound that was somehow familiar. It was Griff's voice. It sounded far off, talking with someone—no, pleading with someone.

Dan spun around to the direction of the voice, but at first couldn't see anything. Then he noticed a foot, protruding out from around the corner. Voices! He heard loud, swearing, violent voices. Dan ran down and cleared the corner.

Griff lay flat on the ground. The same three youths that they had encountered before were kicking and pummelling the man. Dan could tell the backward man had already been seriously injured by this vicious attack.

Dan pulled the nearest thug around and punched him twice to the face. The boy reeled backward, before falling over Griff. Another youth threw a haymaker at Dan, but he easily avoided it. He punched the boy hard on the chin, and sent him crashing to the ground.

This was Dan's second fight in a couple of days. But the fight before this had not been a street fight, but a professional contest. Dan had won that match after six rounds, but the cut on his eye had opened up again—and this time it couldn't be repaired. The injury ended all of Dan's hopes and dreams, and his promising boxing career went down in flames. That was a long time ago though, but he hadn't lost any of his fighting ability over the years. He had easily outfought this trio of punks so far.

The third youth and ringleader, Fred Kelly, managed to kick Dan hard on the leg. It hurt badly, and Dan flew into a rage.

"You want some of this?" Dan shouted, as he spun around and kicked the youth hard on the groin.

The enraged Kelly charged Dan, but then the delayed pain from the kick set in and he doubled-over. Dan wasn't finished with him yet though. As Kelly fell to his knees Dan punched him hard on the nose. The thug fell screaming to the ground.

The first youth was back on his feet now, and snuck behind Dan. He managed to punch him on the side of the face, but Dan spun around and responded with an uppercut that smashed into the young mans chin. This sent him crashing into a heap. The three youths lay on the hard cold ground, squirming in pain, and groaning loudly.

Dan went to the badly injured Griff. "Are you alright, Griff?" he asked. Dan tried to help the bleeding man up.

"Griff ha-has no mo-money," Griff stuttered.

"Take it easy, son," Dan said, and he pulled Griff into an upright position. He leaned him against the wall. There was a serious cut on the top of Griff's head that was bleeding badly, and Dan knew he had to stop the blood loss. He held his handkerchief over the injury, and placed Griff's own hand on it.

"Push on this as hard as you can, and I'll be right back," Dan promised.

He sprinted back to the police station, frightening an old woman as he charged passed her.

"Griff's been hurt bad," he shouted as he entered the station. "Blair, do you have a car I can borrow?"

Blair threw Dan his own set of keys.

"The blue one," he answered. "Take it!"

Dan jumped into the car, unconcerned that it was right hand drive and drove off, wheels spinning. He pulled up alongside Griff.

"C'mon, lets get you inside the car," Dan said, fumbling with the door handle as tried go get Griff into the back seat of the car. Griff could hardly move and Dan could feel his own knees buckle. The guy was heavier than he looked, and it took all Dan's strength to wrestle him in.

Kelly, the ringleader, had gotten to his feet now. He wiped his bloodied nose. As Dan attempted to load Griff into the back of the car, Kelly snuck behind him with a brick in his hand.

Dan saw the boy's reflection in the side mirror, and spun around quickly. Kelly dropped the brick and ran off into the darkness.

When Kelly finally stopped running, he was breathless, and just outside the village, over Ironmills Bridge.

"I'll get that bastard. I'll get him and kill that damn half-wit too," he whispered to himself.

Then Kelly thought he heard someone nearby. He hunkered down, afraid.

The bushes beside him rustled, and he could just make out a figure coming through them.

*The angry Yank has caught up with me*, Kelly thought. *I am going to get another bloody beating.* The youth was spent, and couldn't run another yard.

"Please mister," Kelly snivelled, "I didn't mean to hurt Griff; it was all Mathew Flynn's idea. He started it, he…"

Suddenly he went silent. This wasn't the man he had fought with. Why this man was enormous. A giant! A ten feet tall giant, that towered over him, and hovered menacingly.

The moon lit up its hideous face. It opened its mouth wide. *Wide enough to fit a damn head in there*, he thought. A thick, green substance dripped from its chin. Its long snake like yellow tongue darted in and out of the mouth.

"Dear God, what in heaven's name are you?" Kelly sobbed, just before the creature bit his face off.

The creature pulled Kelly's arms from their sockets. His blood flowed like a burst water main, and his body convulsed and twitched violently. The creature stared down at Kelly for a moment, head bowed, and hissed loudly. Then, it threw its head into the air and sniffed at the light wind that was caressing the trees with its cold breath.

Then, as quickly as it had appeared, the creature was moving back into the dark forest, up into the trees, wailing loudly.

Dan sped off toward the hospital, wheels spinning. He knew Griff needed urgent treatment, and he pushed the car for all it was worth. The quick thinking Blair had already rang the hospital to have them ready for their arrival.

# CHAPTER 16

The two ministers entered the Mine cautiously; the powerful lamps held in their hands as they struggled to illuminate the place fully. Donald and Tully had been forbidden to enter the mine while the blessing was taking place. So they removed the large cross from the trailer, and hid it behind a large rock. The ministers had already decided to work separately, one on each side of the mine. Blessing the entire mine would take about a half-hour to complete. *Not ideal,* the old cleric thought. But it would be enough for their purpose.

Rev McLeay had just started his blessing, when he turned around, and seemed puzzled.

Rev Collins stood with his back to him, far into the corner. He was chanting something in Latin, repeating the same verse over and over again. The old Minister had never heard these words used before, and most definitely, never in a blessing.

A sound echoed loudly across the top of the mine.

Outside Donald and Tully could hear the chanting, but merely thought it was all part of the ritual. Donald radioed the station to make sure the men were paying attention to the cameras, and felt better when they contacted him to report seeing no movements near the mine.

Donald knew the dangers if the beast returned. They would have no chance of escape should it find them. Yet they had to take that chance, and complete this task. There was simply no other way.

Deeper inside the forest, the captain led his group of men across the rain-soaked terrain. The army unit was unaware of the police operation going on at the mine and the captain wasn't really happy about the way the police had been handling things. He felt they weren't sharing information with the military.

*But the Army doesn't need them anyway*, the captain thought. *We will sort this one out, the way we always do. This unit is capable of handling any situation that fate throws at us.*

"Captain," one of his men said, and pointed high "There's something up in that tree."

Although camouflaged, it was quite clear to all it was a camera.

"There's another one, over here sir," a corporal shouted.

"What in bloody blue blazes is going on here?" asked the bewildered captain.

Back at the station Francis was frantically radioing Donald.

"Sir, there is a group of soldiers, camera's six and sevens location. We've been spotted."

"But I left instructions with Sergeant McGrath to inform the army to stay away from the forest; this area is out of bounds to the ar…"

Donald stopped in his tracks, angry, as he realised that Sergeant McGrath had given no such information. He had chastised the sergeant over his treatment of Tully, and the sergeant had then ignored his orders. And now these men's lives were in danger because of it.

He would deal with McGrath later.

"Get on the phone to the military, Francis," Donald commanded. "Order them to get their men to hell out of here immediately!"

Francis was about to redial the military, when she saw something in the top corner of one of the monitors. Something big!

The soldiers on the screen were mulling about, unaware of the presence directly above them.

A young soldier sensed a movement in the bushes, and went over to investigate.

"You poor little mite," he muttered at the small rabbit which was caught in a spring-loaded trap. The trap's sharp metal teeth had snapped tightly shut on the rabbit's rear leg. The leg was badly mangled, but the rabbit looked alert.

It lunged at him, and tried to bite him when he released it.

"You ungrateful little rat ass," he laughed, as the rabbit quickly limped away. *Since when did rabbits suddenly try to bite people?* he thought.

As the soldier turned to re join the others, he staggered back with fright.

"No, please" he moaned, as he moved slowly backward, tripping over the trap from which he just released the rabbit. A tree stopped him from falling onto his back and he flung his arms out behind him, clinging tightly onto the rough bark.

"Wh-what do you w-want with me?" the soldier stuttered to the giant creature.

It hovered before him, head moving from side to side. Then it closed in!

Back at the mine, the older minister was becoming frightened and concerned. Rev Collins was chanting louder. The strange words echoed through the old minister's head.

"What are you doing, George?" he asked, as his own voice came echoing back to him.

"George, George, George," the echo answered.

The young minister stood trance-like, and continued to ignore the older man.

Then in the distance, a sound could be heard. It sounded like a train, far off, but getting nearer and louder.

"What, in the name of all that is true, is happening here?" Rev McLeay asked.

"Happening here, happening here…" the echo answered.

All the while the noise of the train became louder and louder. The old minister, lamp held high, bravely walked deeper into the mine, toward the sound before him. The wall of the mine had come alive, moving violently.

As the Rev McLeay backed away, he could see why. Bats! Thousands of them, But they didn't sound like normal bats. They somehow sounded like an old steam locomotive as they flapped and squeaked.

Rev McLeay turned to run, but Collins blocked his way. His face was red and wrinkled. Something black and worm-like came out from between his lips, wriggled up his cheek, and disappeared into his ear.

"What in God's name are you?" the old minister shouted. "I have been sent by my God, Cernunnos."

"Cernunnos, Cernunnos," the echo answered." I am from the light, but create darkness. I make peace and create evil. I, do all of these things."

"I know of you," the old minister said. "You are Diabolos, the slanderer."

Collins raised his arms and the bats flew at the old man. There were hundreds of the vile animals about him, biting and scratching. He flailed his arms about, trying to fight them off, but there were much too many. Rev McLeay soon fell to his knees, bleeding.

Suddenly the bats flew off him and formed two lines across the mine. Collins walked slowly between their ranks, like some general on parade, and approached the old man. Now he possessed a limp that the old minister hadn't noticed before.

"Here, you kneel to the one true Master," Collins said.

"There is but one Master, you foul abomination. God is the only true Master," the old minister choked.

"Then where is your God now?" Collins scowled." Why is your God not here to help you?"

"Help you, help you, help you," the mine echoed.

"My God is here, don't worry. As long as there is a breath in my body—he's here.

Collins drew a long knife from behind his back and held it menacingly above his head.

"I will spare you if you ask forgiveness from Cernunnos, the one true God," Collins said.

"True God, true God, true God" the echo repeated, but in a different, deeper rasping voice.

"There is but one true God, The Lord God almighty," the old minister answered loudly.

"Haw, haw, haw, the mine echoed.

Donald thought he heard an argument going on. The raised voices coming from the mine instinctively told him that something wasn't right here.

He waved to Tully, and the two men approached the entrance to the mine and peered through the opening.

Donald, gun in hand, cautiously moved inside, as Tully guarded the entrance.

"What in God's name," he declared, as he looked upon the rows of bats crossing the cave-like interior, suspended in midair.

"Then die for your God," Collins screamed as he lunged the knife down into the old minister's chest.

"Die, die, die, you fucker" the echo repeated.

Collins wrenched the red stained knife back out, blood dripping from the blade. He was about to strike again, when two shots rang out, and his head almost exploded as the bullets ripped through him. Blood poured from his head, and ran down his body, onto the floor.

Yet, Collins stood firm, knife raised, and turned to face Donald. His head was cocked to one side and red bloody streaks covered most of his white face. "Who are you that defile's Cernunnos?" Collins asked, as he lowered the knife and widened his twisted mouth. He smiled at Donald, but it was not a pleasant smile. It was a frightening horrifying grin that spewed forth pure evil. "Do you know your wife dies inside, a little more with the passing of each hour?" he sneered. "Soon Heather will join us in Hell."

Collins laughed through blackened, broken, bloody teeth. He raised the knife once again, and Donald aimed his gun carefully, firing off another round. It struck the evil man's heart, and this time he fell heavily in a heap.

As his body hit the ground, the bats panicked and flew out of the mine. It was several minutes before the last bat escaped. When Tully entered he could see Donald propping up his uncle, with the smoking gun still in hand.

"You must let me finish with the blessing of this mine while I still can," begged Rev McLeay.

"But you're hurt, and you need treatment, fast," Tully said.

"I'm all right. Something must have happened to Rev Collins in Africa. The evil must have gotten into him somehow," the old minister coughed.

*What did he mean; Heather dies inside?* Donald thought.

"Help me to my feet," the old minister groaned, and Tully held the brave old man up.

"I will contact the station," Donald said, as He ran back outside to use the radio. The old minister, held up by Tully, continued to bless the mine.

# CHAPTER 17

As Dan sped the car along the dark deserted road, he looked into the rear view mirror. His eye's widened with disbelief as he saw Griff sitting upright in the seat. There was no blood on him, and he was talking to something shiny in his hands. An oblong, glittering object, which looked like gold. Dan hadn't heard this strange language before, and it frightened him.

Suddenly Griff's eye caught him, and Griff smiled. Dan almost ran the car into a ditch as he momentarily lost control.

"Do not be afraid Dan," the voice said.

But Dan was very afraid now, and he pushed the pedal harder to the floor.

"Just who the fuck are you?" Dan said, as he thought about the object in Griff's hands. *Some sort of weapon maybe. A dagger perhaps.*

"I am the messenger," Griff answered.

"Jesus Christ," Dan whined, as he flung the car heavily into the corners.

"I have broken bread with Jesus, along with many other holy people. I visit many good souls in times of evil," Griff went on.

Dan could feel the sweat running down his brow. *What is happening here*, he thought. *Who is this damn maniac?* He was in a panic mode now. Here was the village idiot, who was injured badly and covered in blood. One minute he can barely speak and he's badly hurt, and now he's healed, all the blood is gone, and he's talking like a Shakespearean actor.

"I know all about you, Danny," Griff said. "I know everything about you."

"What things?" Dan asked nervously.

"Well, I know that when you were twelve years old your father told you to stay away from the railway lines. But you disobeyed him, and took your dog, Red, for a walk along the tracks. When you got to the tunnel, Red ran inside. You were both unaware of the train running through. When the train passed, you knew that Red had been killed. You recovered Red's mangled body and buried him beside the rails. Then you went home and lied to your parents. You said that the dog had run away. Your father searched for five days for that dog, and it almost broke his heart."

Dan slowed the car down, almost to a crawl. No one knew about Red and what had happened, absolutely no one. Dan had never told anyone about it, not even Lynn.

"How do you know about *THAT?*" he said. No one knew, and Dan still felt guilty about it, even after all these years.

"It's as I said, I know everything about you, Danny."

Dan didn't like being called "Danny." He'd never liked it, and hadn't been called it since school. Some of his relatives still named him Danny, to try and make him remember his place, like he was still a little boy. When anyone called him Danny though, he usually ignored them. Yet, he felt compelled to listen to this guy.

"Then there was the time in college," Griff went on, and Dan stopped the car. "Let me show you." Griff leaned forward and held out the gold object. This was the item he been speaking to just moments before.

A light swirled up from the object's centre, like a small tornado, and swirled around. Inside the light Dan could the corridor of his old school, with rows of lockers stacked along each side.

> *A young boy walked past, and Dan recognised him. It was himself when he was young. He watched as the boy opened four of the lockers with a skeleton key he had borrowed from a friend, leaving the doors to swing open.*

"I don't want to see this," Dan moaned as the memory of it came flooding back to him. "Please don't!"

But Griff ignored him, and the light swirled more intensely.

> *Then young Dan approached another locker. But this time he knew what he was looking for; as he quickly removed a wallet, from inside and scurried of down the corridor.*
>
> *The wallet with the two hundred and fifty dollars in it belonged to his friend Trooper. It was to pay for a down payment on a scooter that Trooper was going to put down after school. He had worked part time at the burger joint, and had saved the money over the past eight months. After he had paid off the deposit, he was going to treat Dan to a coke and fries.*

*Dan sat in the toilet cubicle and counted the money. It would be his first date tonight with Dempsey, and the twelve dollars he had scrounged from his mother wouldn't have covered cab fair, let alone anything else. He had been asking Dempsey for a date since as far back as he cared to remember, but she had always turned him down. Now though, she had finally said yes. Financially, she couldn't have picked a worse time, but he never imagined that she would actually ever say yes to a date with him. Dan was not going to throw this chance away with the beautiful, full figured cheerleader. Why, dating her was the dream of every boy in the school.*

*He felt bad about taking Trooper's money, but he would feel a damn sight worse if he took Dempsey out with only twelve lousy dollars in his pocket.*

*Dan could imagine coming to school the next day as Dempsey's friends giggled and laughed at him in the corridor, behind his back. "Danny the cheapskate," they would say, and that would be the end of his romance with Dempsey. Now though, it looked as if it would be a date to remember, and he would spend every dime on her.*

*As he stepped from the cubicle, Dan caught a glimpse of himself in the mirror, and he didn't like the reflection that was looking back at him. Trooper had worked hard for this money, and he knew that the scooter had meant everything to him. Trooper was also his best friend in the world. When he had the accident that fractured his leg and was hospitalised for two weeks, Trooper never missed a visit. These visits cheered him up better than any therapy could have done. Dan suddenly felt overwhelmed with guilt, and he stared hard at the mirror for a full minute.*

*'Why did I even think of doing something like this to Trooper?' he whispered to himself. His moment of selfish madness had gone now. To hell with this date with Dempsey, he thought. Even if we did have a great time, how am I ever going to afford future dates after this anyway?*

*'I just can't do it,' Dan said, and he rushed from the toilet. He would just be honest with Dempsey, take his chances, and if she didn't like it—then it was tough. But he couldn't steal from his best friend. In fact, he had never stolen before, ever. And now here he was, the biggest thief of all time. He would have to hurry and return the wallet, before he was seen.*

*When he turned out into the main corridor though, his heart almost stopped. Two of the other boys whose lockers he had opened, were talking to Mr Millar, the vice principle.*

*And as Dan walked passed the vice principle stopped him. 'Hello Danny ,have you seen anyone acting suspiciously in this area?' he asked.*

*'I found this around the corner,' Dan lied, as he handed the wallet over. 'I don't know who owns it,' he lied again.*

*Suddenly, from around the corner, Trooper appeared. 'Any luck, Sir?' he asked.*

*'Why yes, young Danny here just found this wallet. Would this be it?'*

*Trooper almost wrenched the wallet from the man's hands, as he pulled it open.*

*'Yes, yes, that's it,' Trooper answered, and he looked suspiciously at Danny.*

*'Show me exactly where you found it, Danny,' Mr Millar ordered.*

*Dan, red faced, led them up the corridor and pointed.*

*'Along there,' he said.*

*'Why that's a dead end, with no way out. Why would someone throw it down there?' Mr Millar asked, and Dan felt his knees buckle.*

*None of the lockers had been forced open and Dan felt as if the finger of suspicion had already been pointed at him. Yet, he had gotten away with it, and the matter was never mentioned again. Then, when he finally did go out with Dempsey, he found her to be a self centred show off, with no conversational skills whatsoever. The date was a damn flop.*

"Why did you show me that?" asked Dan, annoyed and humiliated. "I've already asked God for forgiveness for trying to steal the wallet."

"Because I wanted you to know that Trooper knew it was you who had taken his wallet all along, but he forgave you, and said nothing."

"No, he never knew, he-he couldn't have," Dan stammered.

"You lost your ring that day, Dan, didn't you? The little silver ring with the dragons head engraved."

"Well, I, I, don't really remember. It was all so long ago. Why, am I meant to remember something like that," Dan groaned, but he knew he had lost his ring that day.

"Well Dan, when Trooper checked on his money, it was not in the same order he had placed it inside the wallet. He always divided it perfectly, by fives, tens, and twenties. There was also something else in the wallet that he hadn't put there either—your ring!"

"Oh God," Dan moaned, putting his hands to his head. Trooper had known all along, but had never mentioned it to him, ever.

"Trooper was your true friend, Dan. He forgave you for it, and so did God, when you prayed to him later that night. When Trooper took his last breath in the isolation ward, you were there with him. This meant more to him than anything you can imagine, and this evened it up."

"Trooper was unconscious, and wouldn't have even known I was there. The doctors said he was brain dead from meningitis," Dan answered, and put his head in his hands.

"Trooper knew!"

Dan felt his emotions swelling up and he looked up to the sky. Confused, his eyes filled with tears. OK, he had done all those things. *But who hasn't done things that no one else knows about. Guilty things,* he thought. Dan was sorry now, but he couldn't change his past, and just had to live with it.

"Who the hell are you?" Dan whispered.

"I am Paul. I am a messenger of the good, but we must go back to the mine. The Beasts and Demons of Baskajira have been summoned. Make haste."

*Beasts and demons*, Dan thought. *Did he just say demons?*

Dan swung the car around, wheels spinning, and headed back toward the mine. Griff touched Dan's shoulder, and immediately he could feel a surge that was almost like electricity. Yet, somehow it soothed him as it shot through his body. He also felt cleansed somehow, as if God had finally forgiven him. Suddenly, Dan was at ease with himself and the choices he had made in his life...

And now, Dan knew they had a chance to beat this thing. Yes, a different kind of power was sitting in the back seat of this car, clothed in the body of a simple-minded man from Cappawhite.

# CHAPTER 18

The young soldier pulled his rifle up from his side, and began firing into the beast. In a few seconds the soldiers had the creature surrounded and they peppered it with gunfire. The creature was moving left to right in quick jerking movements now as the men blasted at it from all directions. Then it sprang forward!

The captain was about to shout another command, when the creature tore his head off in one mighty movement, before hurling the corporal high into the trees. Then most of the other soldiers dropped their weapons and scattered as the beast moved in pursuit of them. The creature tore through the branches as the men tripped and charged along the rough hedgerows in blind panic.

"Hellllp meee," the voice of one of the soldiers pleaded as the beast pulled him up through the branches, and tore violently at his torso.

Bryson, a gunner, didn't panic like the rest of them. His training just wouldn't let him, and if he was to die, then it would be with his full faculties, bravely and with some kind of dignity. He would not beg or scream hysterically.

The bright moon appeared between a clearing in the clouds, and Bryson took careful aim into the tree where the creature was silhouetted. It was still tearing at the thrashing soldier, when Bryson fired the burst.

"Got you, you bastard," he yelled, as the beast dropped the dead soldier and fell back into the branches. "Got it, sar…"

Then seemingly from nowhere, the beast was in front of him, hissing. It drew its head back and Bryson thought he almost detected a laugh. He instinctively fired off another thirty rounds into its chest. Then he stopped, threw the empty machine pistol to the ground and pulled out his revolver. He had barely time to aim it when the frenzied creature set upon him.

Privates McGreevy and Funston had run for all they were worth, and they soon found themselves in a ditch. It was flooded with water, and the men felt the coldness of it penetrating their clothing as they waded knee deep through it. McGreevy had dropped his weapon about five hundred yards back, but Funston clung to his like a man possessed. They had heard the shooting and the screams of the dead and dying behind them.

McGreevy shook with cold and fear. His voice was barely audible and quavered, "Its going to fucking kill us! We're dead men."

"Shut up, just shut up," Funston whispered. "If we keep quiet, it might not notice us."

The two men lay on the bank of the freezing ditch, and prayed.

Then the hedge at the top of the ditch shook, and some twigs flew up from it.

McGreevy crossed himself vigorously. It's got us, Tom."

"Will you shut the fuck up," Funston shouted, angry at this coward who was going to give their position away, and get them caught and murdered. Funston raised his rifle and took careful aim at the hedge. McGreevy pushed his way past, behind him and crouched down.

Then the figure came through the hedge and Funston lowered his rifle.

It was Cummings, the youngest corporal in the regiment. He was badly hurt, and bleeding.

"Are you all right?" Funston asked.

"No, he's not all fucking right," McGreevy chirped in. "Look at the state of him."

"I think my arms broken," the corporal said. "The bloody thing threw me up into a tree."

In the distance the screaming stopped, and an eerie silence crept over the forest.

"It's searching for the rest of our men," Funston said.

"You mean its searching for us, don't you?" McGreevy groaned.

"If you don't shut up, I'll fucking shoot you myself," Funston threatened. Just then a cloud covered the moon, and the ditch moved into darkness. The young corporal pointed into the sky, unaware that he was using his injured arm. He seemed to feel no pain.

It floated about one hundred yards away, coming toward them. Although practically invisible, they could still make out its silhouette.

Then the beast was over them. The three soldiers stayed on their stomachs in the muddy water at the bottom of the ditch, unmoving.

The creature hovered over the ditch, and as the moon once more broke through the clouds, the men witnessed it. It was sniffing at the air, and slowly turning full circle.

"Good God," McGreevy moaned.

The corporal made a violent slashing movement at his throat toward McGreevy, to warn him to shut up, but the shaking man was hysterical, and ignored him.

McGreevy splashed up from the water, and moved quickly up the side of the ditch, ripping out tufts of grass from the sloping bank as he did so.

Funston grabbed for his legs, but McGreevy was too quick, and he had soon disappeared over the top of the ditch.

Then the creature followed quickly over the heads off the men, and passed out of sight. They could hear the creature killing McGreevy, though now his voice made no sound. It was the cracking of his bones and the tearing of his flesh that gave away his fate.

Then the beast moved on, and for now at least, the two soldiers remaining were safe. Then a familiar noise in the distance reached their ears. It was air support. The men instinctively knew the chopper was slowly coming in their direction, as the buzz became louder. A beam of light came shining through the trees, and moved from left to right across.

"If that damn searchlight picks up on us, then we're dead men," the young corporal whispered to Funston.

"We're dead anyway. How long do you think it's going to be before it comes back and finds us?" Funston replied.

Suddenly the helicopter turned and flew off.

Darren Gregg swung the chopper around in an arc as Neil, the co-pilot, pointed frantically through his side window.

"I seen something back there," he reported.

The young pilot had only been flying for two years, but he was fast earning a reputation as one of the best pilots in the chopper squadron.

"I see it, too," Darren answered through his microphone.

He hovered above a large patch of trees, and guided the searchlight over their tops. The strong beam arced around, catching sight of a large figure in its centre.

"My God," Neil croaked. "What is this thing?"

"I don't know, but it's coming up the light," Darren warned.

Darren almost turned the helicopter upside down, as he swung to his right and throttled up.

"Kill the light, kill the light," he shouted.

Then the chopper was quickly moving away.

"What was that fucking thing?" Neil asked through his intercom.

"I don't know, but we're not waiting around to find out."

Then a movement caught Neil's eye, and he looked behind. Something large was moving along the structure, clawing its way along the fuselage of the chopper, toward them.

"It's here!" Neil shouted.

Darren bucked the helicopter up and down, and from side to side, but the creature hung on. Only now it was at the side window, and Darren knew that this was a time for drastic action.

"Hang the hell on," he shouted, as he dived down toward the trees.

Darren would fly the body of the craft through the branches, trying to ensure that the blades didn't touch them. He would force this fucker off!

The creature's mouth was open now, and as it stared in at the men, a yellow tongue rolled behind its teeth.

"Christ," Neil croaked, as he leaned across toward the pilot, away from this nightmare.

"Hang on," Darren yelled as he flew the body of the chopper through the top branches. The windscreen cracked, and the shudder of the craft almost tore them from their harnesses. Some warning alarms sounded, but the chopper flew on, creating a cascade of broken branches and leaves, as it cleared the trees.

"It's gone," Neil said as he looked behind him.

They would clear the forest, and manage to land the badly damaged craft, which was now flying erratically. The young pilot nursed the crippled chopper along. One hundred feet above the trees he flew, hazard lights flashing as warnings continued to buzz.

Then there was a sound—a ripping tearing sound of metal and popping bolts. The chopper lurched. Parts of the fuselage were being torn off from below and it drowned out all the buzzers. The floor was being pulled back like someone opening a giant can of sardines, and the men could see the treetops below through it. The hole below them was big enough to pull three men through it, and the seats were only still held in place by heavy crosspieces. The craft shook violently, and both men knew the chopper was about to rip apart at any second.

"Take her down, for God's sake, take her down," Neil screamed, as the cold night air blew in around them.

The creature somehow came in to the cockpit, behind them. It pulled the young pilots head back and bit into his neck, almost severing it. Blood spurted across the cockpit.

Neil pushed at the stick, and dived. The chopper shuddered and shook. The control panel was flashing all over as more and more warning lights came on, and the alarms sounded more shrilly. Neil didn't want to die and leave his young family, but if he was going to die, then he would die the way he chose, and not from this abomination.

*If I die, at least I am taking that fucker with me,* Neil thought.

The chopper dropped quickly, as Neil forced it into a speedy dive, and just as it was about to hit the ground, he took one last look around. The creature was gone. He pulled frantically at the stick.

"Up, up, up…please," he cried. "Too late!"

The loud explosion nearly deafened the men in the ditch. And the large ball of flame shot up into the night sky like a thousand bright lights, almost blinding them.

"Poor bastards," Funston groaned.

# CHAPTER 19

Rev McLeay exclaimed, "It's done! The blessing is complete! We must leave now." The old man coughed, and winced in pain.

Tully dragged the wounded minister from the mine entrance, as Donald listened intently to the message he was receiving. Then he dropped the radio and yelled to them. "It's coming back! It's returning, please hurry!"

The three men slipped behind a large rock, about twenty feet from the mine entrance. They hardly dared to breathe; as they listened to the last dying echoes of gunfire, and the loud explosion that filled the forest. The screams of the dying men were all too familiar to Tully, and he stared hard at his two horrified colleagues.

At the station, Sergeant McCann, Francis, and the other constables were glued to the monitors, and saw the demon tear some of the soldiers apart. It hovered over one of the cameras, but since they had no cameras pointing at the mine itself, all they could do was wait and pray. Donald had been warned by radio that the beast was coming back to the mine. Everyone at the station began to pray together that the beast would not see the men.

The old minister moaned and struggled to breathe. He pressed tightly against the wound that was now bleeding very badly. Donald urged him to be quiet, as Tully peered out past the large rock.

Then suddenly, it was there. It appeared, even bigger and more menacing looking than before, as it hovered at the mine's entrance.

Donald leaned over Tully's shoulder and sneaked a look. This was the first time he had seen one of these creatures in thirty-five years. This one was much larger than the one Otis had fought though.

*A bloody, great giant of a beast. Perhaps nine or ten feet tall*, he guessed. *And as broad as a damn grizzly bear.*

"Dear God," Tully whispered. "Help us now Lord, we ask of You."

The giant creature stopped about five feet from the mine's entrance, and sniffed at the air. It was hovering about four feet off the ground, and it turned slowly around in a full circle.

Tully held his hand over his uncle's mouth as the man groaned in pain from his wound. Tully prayed the beast wouldn't hear him.

Donald had his revolver at his side, but he would not even try to use it on the creature. No, he had just three bullets left. If the thing discovered them, then he would shoot Tully, the old minister, and then himself. Under no circumstances though, would he let it take them alive.

A badger darted out from the bushes, and scampered passed the beast, disappearing into the far hedge. This giant of a creature that was once

Otis, seemed to study the badger's movements for a moment, as it sniffed at the air. Then slowly it moved on, into the mine.

"Quickly!" Donald urged Tully as he dragged the large cross from its hiding place.

The men struggled with the heavy cross, but were in luck. The cross-slotted in beautifully to the wooden beams on each side of the mine entrance, and the two men pushed at it until it was jammed fast.

The beast could sense something on the floor of the mine, as it hovered above the dead body of Rev Collins. Somewhere inside its mind, its instincts for self-preservation kicked in. There was danger here, everything felt different. It moved upward toward the roof of the mine.

"Let's get the hell out of here," Donald ordered

Tully pulled at his uncle's shoulders, but the old man did not respond. A panicked, sorrowful look ran across his face. He put his head to the old man's chest. There was a faint sound of a heartbeat.

"He's dead Tully," Donald said. "Leave him."

Tully thought about his father and how brave he had been, trying to save those men in the fire, and the consequences of his actions. Actions that had ruined his father's life. Yet, Tully felt certain that his brave father would have done it all over again, if he had been in the same position.

*This is the nature of the beast that calls itself life*, he thought. *Things could be running along quite happily and peaceful, but in one second that same peaceful existence can be ripped to hell. When these things happen, you have two choices: run or fight!*

Tully chose to fight. "No, he's not dead, he's still breathing. You have to help me," he pleaded.

Donald was afraid. And in his fear he was about to run, leaving the other two men behind. But he fought with his fear as brave men do, and instead he stepped back over to them.

"Get his other arm," he ordered Tully, and the two men pulled the old minister to his feet.

From inside the mine, a great wailing and screaming started. The beast inside was struggling toward the exit. Skin ripped and fell from its body. It tried to push the cross from the entrance, but its hands burned and shredded. A terrible heat drove it back inside.

"It's working!" Donald said. "It's really working."

Donald ran across to pick up the radio he had discarded earlier, as Tully held on to this uncle.

"You are not dead, are you uncle?" Tully whispered into his ear.

Rev McLeay opened one eye, and gave a half smile. "Not yet Tully, not by a long chalk," he groaned.

Donald smiled as he contacted the station. "We have it trapped," he announced into the radio "It's in the mine, dyin…" Suddenly he lowered the radio to his side, stopping in his tracks.

Behind the other two men, high in the night sky, the creatures came. There was a large group of them, demons just like Otis, though smaller in size. These abominations were coming for them.

Donald sank to his knees and pointed, as Tully craned his neck to look around. Donald removed his revolver and checked the ammunition.

Somehow the story of a Zulu war entered Tully's mind.

*The brave outnumbered garrison at Rourke's Drift had just killed hundreds of Zulu warriors, and were about to celebrate their astonishing victory—when thousands of Zulu's appeared suddenly above them on the surrounding hills. However, the Zulu warriors did not attack the small garrison. Instead they saluted the soldiers from atop the hills, singing to them and tapping their shields for these brave men. Then they marched away, sparing them.*

Tully knew that this was different though. There would be no saluting here. No singing or sparing of lives either.

"Pray for us, uncle," Tully asked.

"It has already been done," answered the old minister.

There were twelve of the creatures, not counting the one in the mine, which was still shrieking loudly.

*Thirteen, bloody unlucky for some. For us,* Tully thought.

One of the creatures flew to the mine entrance. It crashed violently into the wooden cross, cracking it down the middle. Yet, the cross held firm. The beast fell to the ground, convulsing.

The three men huddled together, as a second creature flew at the cross. It also cracked wood of the cross, but it, too, fell shaking to the ground.

"They are willing to sacrifice themselves to save the one in the mine," Donald stated.

Suddenly a terrific crash issued from the mine entrance, as the largest creature burst out, through the heavy wood, sending pieces of the smashed cross flying in all directions.

The creature was almost naked, as it turned to face the men, but it was truly awe-inspiring. Ribs protruded from its sides that were as thick as a normal man's arms. Its massive chest was broad as a Rhinoceros, which heaved under the beast's laboured breathing. Skin had been ripped off most of its body in patches, and the beast shrieked with pain.

*Now, it was payback time. Our turn to suffer,* Donald thought.

The demon, that once had been Otis Tweedy, squared up to them. Rev McLeay, although badly wounded, forced himself in front of the other two men. He held his bible out toward the creature. The large beast turned away from him, and hissed loudly at one of the others.

Without warning, a smaller creature flew across to old cleric, swiped the bible from his hand, and sent it flying into the bushes.

The large creature, once again, swung around to confront the men.

"Otis," Donald said loudly.

The beast convulsed, snarled and hissed at him.

"Why, Otis, why?" Donald continued.

The creature cocked its head to one side.

"Why do you wish to harm us, Otis?"

"The bloody beast understands you," Tully whispered.

Donald raised his hand for Tully to be quiet. He talked on as the other creatures gradually descended, surrounding them.

"Sarah wouldn't have wanted this, Otis. For pity's sake, think of Sarah! Think of Sarah!" Donald shouted.

The beast shuddered violently for a second; then it bowed, almost as if in prayer.

"It's listening to you, Donald," Tully said. "Keep talking to it."

Then the creature wailed at the men. So loudly they felt their eardrums were about to burst. The other creatures bared their teeth and moved toward them. The three men joined hands and waited, waited for death.

"WE are here," Paul said. Dan hit the brakes hard and the car skidded to a stop.

*I have to help them, I have to try,* Dan thought as he sprinted down the embankment that ran alongside the mine entrance, and almost fell on his face.

In a moment though, he found himself looking up at the awesome brute, up into its hideous face. Dan nearly collapsed in fear at the sheer size of the beast. His hands shook violently, and his knees buckled. *This was real. This was evil at its purist form,* he thought.

*David and Goliath,* he thought. *But this David has no sling shot, no hope.*

The creature seized Dan by the arm and lifted him close up to it, spewing a sort of green mucus all over his face. It stared hard at Dan for a moment, before it opened its huge jaws.

*Oh please, God, no,* Dan thought. *It's going to bite my fucking head off.*

"Otis, please don't do this, Otis," Donald cried. "It doesn't have to be this way."

The yellow tongue like organ in the creatures mouth juddered from side to side, and Dan knew what it was about to do.

Donald felt his whole body shake as he watched Dan try to wriggle free. He had seen Otis butchered by the creature, and now he was about to witness Dan being killed in an even more horrifying way.

But Dan wasn't finished yet. He remembered the little totem, the medicine circle, and he pulled it up from his neck and shoved it into the beast's face.

The creature pulled its head back and wailed. Dan punched it five times to the face with his free hand, but he was like a fly tickling a rhino. Then Tully sprang forward, leaving Donald to support the old injured cleric. Tully leapt up, and punched at its head. Between the two men, vicious blows reigned onto its face. The creature didn't even flinch though, and it tossed Tully away like a rag doll. Tully landed at Donald's feet, but he wasn't hurt and quickly sprang to his feet. Dan kept squirming, trying to free himself. He broke off the chain from the totem, and quickly rammed it into the creature's mouth. Dan cut his hand on its pointed black teeth, but managed to pull it back out.

Dan was flung to the ground, as the creature struggled to remove pendant from its mouth. It ignored him, all the while screaming frantically, as the unknown force from the totem burned its mouth. Finally, the beast was able to spit the totem out. Snarling, it then turned to confront the men once more.

"It's no use," Tully said. "We're done for!"

Donald pulled the revolver up to shoulder level, behind his two colleagues. He would despatch the Rev McLeay first, then Tully. He would do it so quickly that the men wouldn't even know what had hit them. Then he would finish himself off. He could do nothing for Dan, but he shouted for him to run.

Dan couldn't hear Donald, because all the demons had joined in a chorus with the first. Their high-pitched wailing echoed all through the forest.

*Better to end it this way than to be torn to shreds by these creatures, or to be claimed by one of them,* Donald thought.

Donald placed the barrel of the gun to the back of the old clerics head, just as the creature's closed in on them.

"God forgive me," he said, as he cocked the hammer.

Somehow he heard his Aunt Dorothy's voice, "*He is with you, Donald. He is with you now.*" she repeated.

Donald lowered the gun, but still held it nervously. "He is with us," he shouted to no one in particular.

Then another, more powerful voice loomed out from behind them. It drowned out the creatures, almost as though it were coming from the loudest stadium speaker.

"Bathraine, it is I, the follower," the deep voice said. The voice also spoke something in what sounded like Latin. There was no panic in the voice, as it lowered its tone and almost preached to the creatures.

"I am Paul, I am the messenger," the voice continued. The man looked like Griff, but did not act like him. He was bravely confronting the creatures, and showing no fear, as he spoke to them.

The circle of beasts drew back in terror as Griff approached them; but the larger one stood firm, teeth bared, its gnarled hand pointing menacingly.

Dan rushed over beside the other three men

"Are you all OK?" Dan asked, still shaking.

"That's Griff," Donald said, stunned. "What's he doing here?"

"No," Dan answered. "He's not Griff. His name's Paul, like the apostle—but not the apostle. It's complicated. Somehow he's been sent to help us."

Donald looked at Tully, and the men gave each other a disbelieving stare.

"It's true. Trust me!" Dan said.

Dan knew they didn't really believe him, but he wouldn't have either, unless Paul had not proven it to him.

Paul approached the men and he gently put his hand on the Rev McLeay's chest, as the beast's stayed back. The old minister was suddenly able to stand upright. The pain was gone, the wound healed.

"Now do you believe me?" Dan said.

The largest of the creatures wailed again, and flung itself at Paul. He held up the gold oblong object he'd shown to Dan in the car, and the beast retreated.

The same small beam of light, revealed to Dan earlier, twisted up from the object like a small tornado. It then burst into thirteen smaller, narrow beams that shot off in ninety degrees angles from the main beam, and into the bodies of each creature.

The light penetrated the skin of the beasts, illuminating their bodies from within. They all glowed with a greenish, horrible light. Then they were flung through air, backs slamming with great force into the outer embankment wall of the mine.

The powerful force held them there. Then that same force swung their arms out from their bodies, legs held firmly down, crucifixion style. Everything was silent now, except for intermittent soft hissing noises that emanated from the beasts. The creatures shook in fear, as if they knew some terrible retribution, their final comeuppance, was about to befall them.

The largest of the beasts, the one that was once Otis, fought hard to free itself. It seemed determined never to give up. It turned and loudly wailed at the others, as if commanding them to try and fight back. Its head rocked violently from side to side, and it snarled and hissed loudly. The other beasts remained still. Resigned to their fate, they lowered their heads in submission.

# CHAPTER 20

Francis shouted, "What is happening to them, Blair?" She tried desperately to radio the men, "Why won't they answer us?"

"Maybe the signal is weak?" Blair answered. "Or maybe the beast got to them."

"I'm going to go get them," Francis said.

"No!" Blair ordered.

Francis ran from the room, ignoring him, grabbing the car keys as she went.

"Wait, Francis, wait," Blair yelled. But Francis had already made her mind up and ran out from the building. Blair took one last look at the monitors and paused for a moment. "God be with us," he said, as he followed after her.

As Francis thrust the keys into the ignition, the passenger door swung opened.

"I'm going with you," Blair stated, revolver in hand.

The car sped off toward Lamont's Mine.

Paul stood in the centre, between the outer face of the mine, and the trees that lined the forest's edge.

He stood, tall and steady, with arms outstretched. He was like some zealous schoolmaster, chastising the boys and girls for not doing their homework. His face showed no emotion as he carefully, in turn, studied each of the creatures.

The largest beast had managed to force its head from the wall, and continued wailing loudly. The rest had remained quiet, and began to shake in their fear.

Paul pulled off little gold triangles from the shining object and walked over to each of the beasts. He pushed the triangles into the sides of their feet, and the creatures gave a shudder. A small trickle of something like dark green blood ran from their small wounds, and flowed to the ground.

When Paul got to the largest one, it swung its head toward him; teeth bared as it snarled viciously at him. A black foam like substance poured from between its lips, and its sickly yellow tongue protruded out over the teeth. Paul passed the golden object over its leg, and the beast shrieked louder than ever before.

Two lights suddenly appeared, from just beyond the first row of trees. Faintly at first, then increasing rapidly in strength, until they were almost blinding. The lights formed sheets, planes that looked like large doorways, about twelve feet high, and just as wide. They had a crystalline structure that sparkled and glistened. One was white in colour, and the other had a hint of brilliant blue. A loud buzzing sound emulated from them, like a trillion bees were waiting to burst forth from them.

The men stood in awe. This power was something they could never have dared to imagine.

Then to Donald's left, two figures suddenly appeared, running toward them. It was Francis and Sergeant McCann.

Francis ignored the others, throwing her arms around Tully's neck.

"Thank, God, you are alright," she said.

Tully looked into her eyes, passed her tears, and at last he knew. He had seen that look before from Francis, but simply put it down to a girl's grammar school crush. Now though, there was no mistake—this was a much bigger, deeper thing.

Tully knew he could feel the same way about her, and he gave her a smile. But they would have to survive this night first before he could do anything with his life. His immediate thoughts went back to the creatures lined up in front of them.

When Paul called out to the first creature, Francis inched back, startled and afraid, as she witnessed the sight before her. But Tully held her tightly.

"Why, that's Griff," she said.

"No, it's not Griff," Tully answered. "He's Paul, the Messenger"

"Asela," Paul called to the first one. "I command you, in the name of God, to give up the stolen ones."

The beast convulsed violently for about fifteen seconds. Then something began to happen.

A small bubble-shaped orb appeared from the creature's chest. The orb was no bigger than an orange, and it broke through the beast's tough skin. Others followed; soon there was a line of orbs moving slowly down, away from the creature.

When the first of these orbs touched the ground, it quickly transformed into a human shape, something made from vapours, a spirit form. The first was a knight. The man's armour glistened as he walked toward, and then through the white door of light. As each orb, in turn, hit the ground, they would turn into these human spirit forms and walk through the white doorway of light.

"Estrivaille," Paul said to the next creature, giving it the same command as the one before it.

There were many different types of these spirit people appearing in front of them now: a Roman Centurion, a Spanish Conquistador, and an old sea captain. All moving quickly on, toward the light in front of them. A U S cavalryman bowed to them, doffed his hat in a sweeping motion, and smiled before exiting.

"Why, they can see us," Tully exclaimed, as Francis held his hand tightly. Suddenly a fine looking Sioux warrior appeared, and danced full circle before them, laughing.

*Satra,* Dan thought, as he waved at the cheerful fellow.

Then a little girl appeared, and waved.

"Emily," Donald said to her, as he wiped away a tear, and the little girl skipped happily away.

A British soldier in full uniform stopped before them and saluted. Donald and Tully saluted him in return. Then he turned smartly, as if on parade, and marched quickly away. Next a young submariner slowly walked past.

"Hans Bachmann?" Dan heard himself say.

The German sailor nodded to him and smiled.

Donald moved forward, as if he was going to shake the sailor's hand, but Paul quickly stopped him.

"You must not touch them," he commanded, and Donald backed off.

"Railshorin, Alusha," Paul went on, as he continued talking to each creature in turn.

And still the orbs continued to come forth. There were orbs coming out of all the creatures now, hundred's of them, almost like soap bubbles. Each returned inspirit to the human form it once had, before entering the white doorway of light in front of them. Souls of people from every walk of life, gathered over hundreds of years by these creatures. Now at last, they were being released, so they could go on to the greater good.

Paul finally approached the largest of them, the one that had taken Otis.

"Bathraine," Paul said, quietly. But before he could say more, the giant creature tore half its body away from the rock face, wailed, and shook its gnarled hand toward his face.

It fought hard to tear its body from the rock wall of the mine, but the small beam of light held it tightly.

Just as the men felt as though their eardrums were about to burst open from Bathraine's piercing wails, the orbs stopped coming from the creatures. Paul pulled the shining object to his side. The lights that were penetrating the creature's chests faded, and the creatures slowly descended to the ground. They were spent now and could hardly stand. A couple of the creatures fell to their knees, and cried pitifully.

The men watched in awe as the larger one, Bathraine, struggled over and placed its arms around the two others of its kind, stopping them from falling to the ground. Although it was clearly very weak, it bravely and defiantly stood to the front of them. It swayed in the moonlight, as it tried to protect them.

*This was some sort of wonderful loyal act of compassion toward its own,* Donald thought, *even though it is a vile cruel monster.*

Paul turned toward the other doorway that no one had entered and said something that no one could understand. Then from behind the blue, diamond-like doorway of light, figures could be seen.

These figures, thirteen in all, walked slowly out from the light and walked toward the mine. They were led by a beautiful young woman with long flowing red hair. As they approached the creatures, Donald instantly recognised her. She was even younger and more beautiful than he had remembered her, but there was no mistaking her.

It was Sarah!

As she approached creatures, she held her arms out and smiled at the largest one.

"Otis," she said.

The large creature convulsed, as the other creature's continued to cry and wail pitifully.

"Otis," Sarah repeated, and the beast slowly held out its large hand. Sarah gently held onto it. It opened its twisted mouth, one last time, and in its torment, it hissed loudly at her. Its head shook violently, and cranked back so far, that the men thought it would somehow detach from the body.

Then the hissing stopped, and its head drew slowly forward again. Suddenly the large creature started to change. Its great ribs were shrinking, as it doubled, folding foetus-like onto its knees, but Sarah held its hand tightly. Its grey skin was slowly darkening. The great rows of black pointed teeth, once so frightening, were now quickly disappearing, and the long tufts of hair were drawn back up into its head. Then suddenly, he stood upright.

Otis! He had no deformity on his face, like he had when Donald first met him, and he looked younger, much younger. Even though it was thirty-five years ago since Donald last saw Otis, there was still no mistaking him either. Otis smiled at Sarah, and lovingly embraced her.

Together, hand in hand, they walked toward the light. As Otis and Sarah passed the men, they briefly stopped. Sarah, smiling, gave a small wave and Otis laughed his Burt Lancaster laugh, as he moved his head in the Burt way, and bowed to the men.

Then they moved back into the blue light, followed by the other creature's who had also transformed. They were also being guided toward the light by their loved ones. And each creature had turned back into the person they used to be.

"They know we helped them," Tully said.

"They sure do," Dan added.

The old minister clasped his hands in prayer, and looked to the heavens, smiling.

"The power of God is surely a wondrous thing," he said.

Dan was wiping the tears away from his eyes, when Paul slowly approached him.

"Come-Dan," he said, "You must come with me now."

# CHAPTER 21

P aul said, "I am going to take you on a journey, Dan, through time and space to show you how certain things are going to be changed."

"Changed?" Dan asked, puzzled.

A heavy white mist appeared before them, and four colours of light leapt from its centre and spiralled up into space, buzzing loudly.

The lights were red, green, blue and yellow.

Paul reached over and held Dan's hand, and smiled. A warm and comforting, trusting smile. Dan felt somehow at ease with this powerful man who had a direct link to God and all things holy.

As they entered the mist, Dan looked around at the group he was leaving behind, and waved at them. He somehow knew instinctively that he would never see them again, and he felt sorrow. In the short space of time that he had been with them, a bond had formed and he would miss them. They were still waving when the mist surrounded him, and then they disappeared.

Paul and Dan entered the red, tunnel-like beam of light first, and were propelled along a shaft. The feeling Dan got was of being submerged in water, but he was still able to breath, and he found himself enjoying the experience.

In a few minutes they came out from the light, and entered a scene that looked like someone was shooting a movie, except there were no cameras to be seen.

They were inside the small, smoke-filled room of a restaurant, but the smoke wasn't coming from cigarettes. The smoke was from cordite. The sulphur stench was unmistakable. There were also two men standing with hoods and guns. A girl lay writhing on the floor, wounded, while a man lay dead further up the bar. Another younger man, his hood half-pulled from his head, lay dead with a knife protruding from his neck.

Suddenly a young Otis burst in, gun blazing. He fired without hesitation, and the other two robbers fell dead, unable to even get a shot off. Then another cop entered the room, gun in hand. It was Lewis.

Even though Dan didn't know Lewis or had never even heard the story about the robbery, he was somehow filled with the knowledge of what had happened before. The first time Otis had failed to shoot, and Lewis his partner was killed.

The past was changing here, and Dan was witnessing it first hand.

"Why would God change the past for these men?" Dan asked, puzzled.

"The forces of good can do anything Dan, anything," Paul repeated. "The power and the wisdom only comes from good. And only God knows the answer to your question. I am but a simple messenger."

"What will happen to Lewis?" Dan asked.

"He who lives, shall be allowed to live. If God decides it, then it will be so," Paul exclaimed.

Dan wasn't exactly sure what Paul was talking about. But he guessed he meant that Lewis would have a great life.

Dan took one last look at the two cops who were embracing each other, and then turned to follow Paul.

They travelled back along the red light and as soon as they came to its end, they immediately entered the blue one. Dan felt like Scrooge as he journeyed with the three spirits. But unlike Scrooge, he felt no fear. He would just sit back and enjoy the ride. On this journey through time, there was no passing of stars or planets. Yet, sometimes lights would soar through the beam. And as they touched Dan's body, a feeling ran through him—a feeling of total joy and well being.

"What you are experiencing is a phenomenon known as the cleansing lights," Paul informed him without actually opening his mouth, but the message came through clearly, filling Dan's brain.

*Who needs ears in this world?* Dan thought. *What I'm experiencing here is telepathy.*

"What are cleansing lights?" Dan communicated back, without talking.

"These lights stop the dark forces from travelling through time. I'm sure you can imagine what would happen if just one of these abominations were to get through. The damage caused would be catastrophic. But these lights you are feeling now are the very breath of God. Nothing passes without the creator's knowledge."

"So God knows I'm here?" Dan questioned.

"God knows," came the reply.

When they emerged from the blue light, they found themselves on the deck of a large liner.

People were milling about all over the place. The sun was shining down, and the sea was calm. Some children were playing hopscotch on the deck, and the way they were dressed made Dan feel it was sometime in the early twentieth century. *The twenties or thirties, perhaps,* he thought.

"Can they see us?" Dan asked.

"No," came the firm reply. "But do not try to touch them."

Paul led Dan across the deck, where a group of women where laughing and joking. The handsome man in their centre was smiling and laughing with them, as his wife clung lovingly to his arm. Paul didn't speak, but he didn't have to. Dan somehow simply knew who they were.

It was old Mick, but now young again. He could see Mick and his wife, Mary, who were accompanied by the rest of his sisters. He had sold the farm, and they were all heading off to America. They would have a great life, Dan knew, and they would prosper.

"I'm overjoyed. Michael," Mary was saying.

"Aye, sure it will be a great adventure Mary," Mick answered, as he leaned over and rubbed young Bridget's head. She, in turn, smiled back at him.

Then Paul and Dan entered the green light, and when they emerged Dan immediately recognised Otis again. They where standing inside the living room of a rather squalid house. Clothes were strewn about, and the floor was covered in empty beer cans and old magazines.

Otis was talking to a woman, while his partner questioned her husband. Then suddenly the man stabbed Otis's partner in the back, and Otis on reflex, shot him twice. Dan watched in amazement as the woman picked up a flare gun and fired it at Otis. But Otis had already heard his partner's warning and had ducked away. The flare hit the corner of the room and some curtains were set alight.

Otis called for back up. The fire was put out and the woman was arrested. Otis would never receive the injury to his face, and he would spend the rest of his working life in the police force.

Then they emerged from the green light, and only the yellow light remained.

Dan was by now starting to really enjoy the experience. *After all*, he thought. *How many times do you get to witness God's work at close hand like this?*

Paul released Dan's hand.

"This light is for you to travel alone, Dan," he said.

Suddenly Dan felt afraid. Travelling through the lights with someone who had been sent from God was just fine, but to travel alone to some unknown time and place was a daunting prospect.

"I-I, don't really want to," Dan stuttered. "I don't want to go alone."

"You must, my son," Paul answered. "Trust in me, and enter the light. Hurry, Dan, before it is too late."

"Alright, I'll do it," Dan said.

"Will I see you again?" he asked.

"Yes Dan," Paul answered. "You will! And much sooner than you think. But you won't recognise me, and you will not remember anything of what you have just witnessed here when you awake. This is Gods will. Goodbye!"

"What about Beatrice, will I ever see her again?" Dan interrupted. "No, your past is going to change. Now go, quickly."

Dan smiled and wished him goodbye. But he had a tear in his eye as he thought about Beatrice. Maybe he loved her more than he realised, and now he became choked up at the thought of never seeing her again. "Will you please ask God to look after her?" he asked.

"This will be done."

Then Dan slowly and with great hesitation, entered the light. Dan immediately felt differently about this light though. He couldn't move and he couldn't breathe. As a child, he had once held his breath under water for a full three minutes, but now he was a lot older. All those years of smoking wouldn't help him now. Suddenly Dan saw a movement at his feet, but he couldn't quite make it out. The cleansing lights were dazzling him. *It looked like a, like a little toy bears head*, he thought. *I must be hallucinating, yeah, that's it.* Then his head went light, and as he closed his eyes, he fell into a deep sleep.

Across in Dublin, Heather was rubbing at her painful side and thinking about her cancer, How was she was going to tell Donald and her loving son that she was going to die? Suddenly she noticed a discolouring in the wall in front of her. It looked like a stain of sorts, but this stain was moving. Twisting and swelling like a mini-tornado. And as she stared at it, she became frightened. Suddenly a roar like a jet plane emitted from its centre, and the wallpaper parted. As she moved to the side, it moved. And when she doubled back, it doubled back.

The damn thing was following her. No, not-following her, she felt. It was lining up with her. And now the damn thing was coming out from the wall.

Heather turned to run, afraid. But before she could take a step, the small tornado sprang from the wall and entered her chest with a thud. Heather was sent sprawling onto the chair, and it was a few moments before she could regain her composure. When she stood up the pain in her side had gone, the room empty and silent. There was no numbness now, and she touched her side in disbelief. Her breathing was no longer laboured, and she felt much stronger. She had not imagined this, she knew, and now she felt cleansed. Heather walked outside and looked into the sky, smiling up to the one being that had cured her.

"Thank you God," she whispered. "Thank you so much.

# CHAPTER 22

Dan opened his eyes and stared at the ceiling for a few minutes before throwing his legs over the side of the bed. He still felt very tired and numb; as if he hadn't had any sleep at all, but he knew he had things to do. The smell of freshly cooked bacon strips and eggs pleasantly wafted up into his nostrils from the kitchen downstairs. He rubbed at his eyes and stretched. Then he stared out from the bedroom window, across the lawn. As the rain lashed against the panes, he wished he could spend the rest of the day at home.

Dan was unaware of all those years he had spent with Beatrice. He wouldn't even have known her now if he were to meet her in the street. Now all those years had, in fact, never happened for him—not since he entered the light and changed his past.

Lynn hadn't driven to work that morning. Hadn't been killed, and they had remained happy together with their two children Tom and Grace.

A woman's voice floated up to him from downstairs, singing, breaking the silence of the quiet morning. His head throbbed, and he remembered having a weird frightening dream of sorts. But by the time he reached the bottom step, he had forgotten that he had even had a dream, and the headache was now gone. Grace, his daughter smiled at him and pointed at his feet, giggling.

"Hi Dad!" she said.

Dan looked down and noticed that his slippers were on the wrong feet, and he laughed with her.

"Hi yourself," Dan said.

"Morning, hon," Lynn said. "I've just cooked us some breakfast."

"Where's Tom?" he asked, yawning, as he placed his arm on her shoulder.

"You just missed him, Dad," Grace commented.

"Shit," Dan said. "I wanted to wish him luck in his new job, dammit."

Dan kissed Lynn goodbye, waved at Grace and drove off toward the office. He was covering a story about corruption in the penal system, and he needed to tie up some loose ends. But he had promised to help Bennett, a junior at the paper, who was covering a story about a Hell's Angels conference in Los Angeles.

Even though it was raining, Dan parked the car some distance away and hurried through the rain. As he neared the entrance, he spotted a figure outside the building, picking litter up from the ground.

"Hello Griff," he shouted to the backward guy, who was rambling away to himself. Griff, as far back as Dan could remember, had always been there, picking up the litter and keeping the place spotless. He was there when Dan had first started at the paper. The uncanny thing was that the damn guy hadn't changed a bit in all those years.

Dan opened his wallet and pushed a ten dollar bill into Griff's hand.

"It's much too cold and wet to be outside on a day like this," Dan said. "Go get yourself a coffee. Are you trying to catch your damn death or something?"

Griff ignored the question, made no eye contact, and tucked the money inside his trouser pocket.

"Th-thank you, M-Mr Winters," Griff stuttered, and walked slowly on, picking up any litter as he went...

"You're welcome, Griff," Dan said as he disappeared through the large revolving doors.

Jackson, the large, bear-like security guard, approached Dan as he entered the warm welcoming interior.

"Hello Mr Winters," Jackson said.

"Now how many times have I told you Harvey? It's Dan, OK, just Dan," he repeated.

"Yeah, OK, JUST-DAN," Harvey said with a laugh.

"I just wanted you to know, I'm retiring at the end of the week."

"Are you bull-shiting me here. Harve?" Dan asked.

"Why no Mr Win...I mean Dan. I leave Friday!"

"I wished I had known," Dan murmured, as he fumbled in his briefcase. "How long have you worked here, Harve?"

"Twenty-five years and some, I guess."

"Twenty-five years, and not one goddamn person in the place mentioned you were leaving. What a sad, fucking company." Dan pretended to walk away, but suddenly stopped and spun round. "Maybe you could drop this letter off for me, Harve. It's quite urgent that the man read it as soon as possible."

"Sure thing Mr Winters, no problem." As Harvey reached for the envelope, he noticed it had his name on the front, in big bold letters. "Why, this let…"

"Maybe this will be of some small help to you Harve," Dan interrupted, as he released the envelope to Harvey, and winked at him.

Harvey impatiently tore at the envelope, pulled out its contents, and stared at the card with all the names inside.

"Happy Retirement!" the card said.

*So many names,* Harvey thought, as he stared at them for a moment, open mouthed. "Why I, I just don't know what to say, Mr-um, Dan."

"You're a well thought of man, Harve. Guys had a whip round for you. Everyone in the building gave."

"I'll say," Harvey exclaimed, as he removed the large cheque attached to the letter.

Then the men hugged each other affectionately.

"You can take Helen on a great vacation now," Dan laughed.

"You bet ya."

"You'll be sorely missed, Harve," Dan said, as he stared at Harvey's sorry looking replacement, and grinned at the buck-toothed kid with the loose fitting uniform.

When he entered his office, a padded envelope lay on his desk, and he tore it open.

"Another one," he whispered, and smiled. The certificate with the gold and marble frame was beautiful, but there was just no room left on any of his walls to place it.

"Wow, another one!" Bennett echoed, as he entered the office, and stared somewhat jealously at the award in Dan's hand.

"Don't you worry, Bennett,. I'm sure you will have just as many by the time you reach my age."

"I should be so lucky," Bennett moaned, as he sat down and waited for Dan's help.

Dan couldn't remember feeling as good about his life as he did now. He had it all, he felt, and life was great.

"C'mon Bennett, lets get this story written."

Next morning, as Dan sat down for breakfast, Lynn toiled busily at the stove.

An old John Wayne movie was showing on the portable television that sat atop the kitchen breakfast bar.

The movie showing was *The Quiet Man*, and John Wayne had just kissed Maureen O'Hara.

The green fields and scenery of Ireland's lush valleys behind them on the screen appealed to Dan.

"You know something Lynn," he said loudly.

"No, what, tell me?"

"I have always wanted to go to that place."

"What place?" Lynn asked, puzzled, as she turned from the stove, her face radiant in the glow from the overhead light.

"Ireland."

"Ireland," she echoed.

"Yeah, Ireland. Maybe we should vacation there sometime."

"Any particular part of Ireland you wish to visit?" Lynn asked.

Dan thought for a moment before answering. He was sure there was a place he had always wanted to go, but for some unknown reason, he just could not remember.

"I was thinking about hiring a car. We could tour all around the place."

"Yeah, that would be fun," Lynn answered.

"I'll go get some brochure's on my way home from the office," Dan said.

"It won't be this year though; Lynn exclaimed. "I'm far too committed at the hospital until then. Can't you maybe wait until next year? I'll have a definite think about it then."

"I can wait," Dan said, smiling. "I can wait."

"They say it's a beautiful country, and the people are so friendly," Lynn exclaimed.

"Yeah, and just maybe we'll see a Leprechaun or a Fairy or two," Dan joked.

"Or maybe a Banshee," Lynn answered, as she made a funny wooing sound.

"Yeah, and maybe if we catch the Leprechaun, the damn little sonofabitch will have to give us three wishes," Dan said, laughing.

"And just what would you wish for, if you had the chance?"

"Well, I would wish that the little guy would give me the will-power to resist your cooking hon. That's what I'd wish for!"

Lynn walked slowly across to him, and held the plate under his nose.

"Now where am I going to put all that stuff?" Dan asked, as he stared at the over-crowded plate, but immediately reached for the salt.

"Just like Mama used to make," Lynn laughed.

"That movie slays me," Dan said, as he pointed at the small television.

"You know, these guy's punch each other over ten times to the face and body and…"

"Why, have you counted each punch then?" Lynn interrupted.

"Yeah, I have. In this movie, the two guys punch each other halfway across Ireland. And they are big guys, McLaughlin and Wayne. And do you know something?"

"No, do I know what?"

"There's not one drop of goddamn blood," Dan stated firmly. "Why just one of those haymaker punches would kill any normal guy. But with these two guys, not so much as a damn nose bleed!"

"Well, it is only a movie," Lynn answered. "Anyway, they thought about children watching back in those days."

"Yeah well, even Otis couldn't beat these guys."

"Who's Otis?" Lynn asked, puzzled.

"Why, I don't know. It just slipped out. Must have been a movie I seen once, I guess."

*Otis,* Dan thought. *Just who the hell is Otis?*

Across the television screen, John Wayne had just faded away, and the two letters covering the small screen lit up brightly.

"The End," the letters said.

# CHAPTER 23

## PRESENT DAY

Back in Ireland, Brian Casey and his twin brother, Charles, had decided to defy their mother for the second time in a week, and go play with friends. Greta had tried her best, but the fourteen year olds had been getting harder and harder to control these past five years. Ever since Ben, their father, had walked out without so much as a by your leave, when the boys were only nine years old.

Ben had simply walked out with the clothes on his back and disappeared, never to return again. He had removed the photographs from his wallet though. Photo's of the children he professed to love, and left them scattered on the bed. *Better he had burned them,* she thought.

It was hurtful for Greta for a long time afterwards; as she fretted for the man she had loved more than anything.

But now!

Now the love she once had for this man had been replaced by a deep seeded hatred. She instinctively knew there was another woman. Someone he had decided to be with and whom he had chosen to make a new life with. A new life where there was no part to play for any of them.

But for the sake of her children, the brave woman had battled on, struggling year after year.

She thought back to the time when her husband had left. There may have been sign's, but nothing that would have made her suspect anything.

Ben had always told her he loved her. Right up until he left. He had also doted on the boys, and had taken them everywhere with him.

Greta just could not believe he had another woman. *Why had he betrayed me like this?* She wondered. They had been childhood sweethearts, and had never had any other partners. *Why didn't someone tell me?* She thought.

But her friend, Robin, had said to her once, that, "The wife's always the last to know, dear."

And of course, Robin had been right.

With regard to the twins, Charles had been the one to cause her the most concern, bullying other boys at school, and stealing their money. Ten times she had been to see the easy-going headmaster, Mr Reid. Ten times in the past two years. Twice because of Brian's behaviour, and eight times over Charles.

Now Charles was on his last legs, and it seemed a forgone conclusion, that he would be expelled from the school at Cappawhite.

Greta had thrashed him when she heard how he had told the headmaster to fuck off. He also had turned on her, and had threatened her with violence. He blamed her for the reasons why the father he loved so much, had run away.

Charles had never lied to her though. Once confronted about any misbehaviour he had been involved in, he simply admitted it. At least Greta had to give him that. Like the one time, the headmaster accused him of taking a boy's sandwich, and brought him to the office. Charles swiftly informed him that it was two sandwiches, and a packet of sweets. Yes, Charles could take his medicine.

Now Greta sat in despair, and cried. Grounding them had done no good. And Charles's influence on his younger twin was growing menacingly worse by the day.

The priest had tried talking to the boys, but Charles had bad mouthed him also.

It was now only a matter of time she felt, that she might also be beaten by Charles. Maybe she would be beaten by the two of them. But the law would brand her an unfit mother, should she leave them, and the shame of facing her neighbour's afterward would be unbearable.

God, she felt, had deserted her, planned this for her. Because no matter how much she prayed, her prayers were never answered.

Something suddenly entered her mind, and she screwed up her face as she tried hard to remember. Remember back to when it had all fell apart for her.

*It was a Saturday night, when Ben had come in, sweating and panting for breath. It was just about one week before he left home. His jacket had been torn, and he had a few light marks on his face. When Greta asked him what had happened though, he clammed up.*

*But she had pushed for an explanation and he had finally told her he had been in a fight, refusing to say any more about it.*

Greta stood up and slowly walked to the kitchen. She had never known Ben to be in a fight before, because Ben didn't fight!

Ben was completely a non-violent person. He wouldn't even watch television if something about war or the like was on.

Now that Greta thought about it, Ben had seemed edgy that day. Since immediately after the so-called fight, and right up until the day before he left, he paced the bedroom floor.

*This was just his guilt trip,* she thought. *He had probably been fighting with the woman's husband. Yes, this was why he had paced the floor.*

Greta roughly pulled her coat from the peg on which it hung, and slammed the door behind her as she left the house. She would go look for her boys, and come hell or high water, they would be returning home with her this night.

It was getting dark now, and she cursed as she stumbled in her haste.

As she hurried down the street, she met Colin Gray, but he lowered his head, and avoided eye contact with the woman whom he always thought to be mad anyway.

Why just last week she had told him to stay away from her boys, or she would make sure he got what was coming to him. She had blamed him for getting her boys into trouble, but he had done nothing of the sort. Now he wouldn't play with them again. He actually felt frightened by this sad unstable woman, and he hurried on. But she had seen him.

"Colin," Greta shouted across to him. "Have you seen my boys?"

Colin had seen them alright, down by Ironmills Bridge, but he was afraid to tell her in case she thought he had been playing with them. She might give him 'the what was coming to him' that she had promised.

"N-no, Mrs Casey, I haven't seen them," he lied.

It had started to rain now, and Greta didn't have her umbrella. But she would not return home without the boys and she quickened her stride. Greta scanned the empty fields at the end of the village, but could see no one.

Then, and out of the blue, a lightning bolt lit up the sky. The crash of thunder that followed almost deafened her.

*Maybe some good can come out of this,* she thought.

If the boys had a weakness, then this was it. Their Achilles heel! Since small boys they had been terrified of storms. Not because of the roar of the thunderclaps either, but because, when they were young children, they had witnessed their friend Oliver being killed by fork lightning. His head was a smoking ball of blackness. His face so badly burnt that no one could recognise him, not even his own mother. The boys had fretted for some time over this, and even the mention of a thunderstorm would put them into a state.

*This storm would drive them home,* she thought.

Old mother Baxter had spotted Greta through her window, and she called to her from the front door, cautiously opening it to about a six inch gap.

"Are you looking for your two boys, Greta?" she called.

"Yes Mrs Baxter, have you seen them?"

The old woman put her frail hand through the gap and pointed toward the bridge, which was about five hundred yards away.

"I saw them about an hour ago. They passed my window."

"Thank you so much, Mrs Baxter," Greta said, and hurried on.

Greta had only moved about twenty yards, when she saw the figure in the distance come staggering toward her. It was Brian, and he was crying.

Greta moved with some speed now, toward the boy, as the lightning and thunder boomed overhead, and the rain fell heavy.

"Where's Charles?" she yelled to the distraught boy. "What has happened to you?"

Brian couldn't speak, but whimpered like some trapped animal that was about to be eaten by its prey.

Greta had no mobile phone with her. In fact, Greta didn't even own a mobile phone, afraid that the school would be constantly ringing her to complain about her son's behaviour.

But they were her boys, and no matter what, she loved them!

Greta roughly dragged Brian back to the old woman's house and vigorously rapped on the door. But the nosey old woman had seen her coming, and was already at the front door. The door cracked open, the usual six inches, but Greta gave the old woman no time to speak.

"Phone for an ambulance Mrs Baxter. Please, phone for an ambulance," Greta repeated.

Just then Constable Fagan drove around the corner at some speed, and the car skidded wildly. He would be finished with his duties in about ten minutes and would be going home for the night, and he was in a hurry. He had been warned twice about his high speed, reckless driving around the country roads, but the warnings had been like water off a duck's back to him.

Greta spotted him though, and ran into the road, waving him down.

*Good God*, he thought. *What the bloody hell's going on here?*

Fagan had promised Jo he would be home early, because it was her birthday, and the sergeant had refused to let the skiving constable take the night off. He had planned to rush home, open a bottle of wine, and then surprise her with the engagement ring he had bought three days previously. Then they could have a little party, just for the two of them. Everything would have been perfect, but now this!

Even before Fagan opened the police car door, he knew his plans were ruined. Something seemed to be serious here, and he would have to deal with it. He would probably be spending half the night doing bloody paper work.

And Jo! Well, Fagan was certain she wouldn't believe him, but what could he do?

As he exited from the car, Greta ran to him. "My boys," she screamed. "My boys!"

"Now just calm down madam," Constable Fagan said, in an abrupt manner.

"Just what's going on here? What's wrong with him?" he asked, pointing at Brian.

What do you think is wrong?" Greta yelled at the Constable. "What the hell do you think is wrong?" she repeated. "Just look at him. Look at him!"

"Calm down, will you madam? You're not helping him any!"

"Look," she said. "Something has scared him very badly, and my other boy, Charles is missing."

"What age are the boys?"

"Fourteen, and they are twins."

Constable Fagan had only been transferred to Cappawhite two weeks previously, and had yet to get to know the villagers. Yet, he suddenly recognised the boy. He had told him and his brother off for having thrown stones at a woman walking her dog, just two days before. And he remembered thinking at the time that he was going to have trouble with these boys.

Fagan was pretty sure of what had happened to them though. Someone had maybe threatened or slapped them about a bit, which was no more than they deserved. But he took one look into the crying woman's face, and his heart filled with pity for her.

The police station was only about three hundred yards away and Constable Fagan radioed for assistance.

In less than two minutes, a burly sergeant appeared from around the corner. The light from the street lamp lit him up, his well-honed toe caps glittered like cat's eyes. He was agitated at having been called out from his warm, dry station, and his voice betrayed him.

"What the hell is it now Fagan?" he growled.

Constable Fagan pretended not to hear him, and only answered when he was almost upon them, "This lady feels something has happened to her boys, sergeant."

"Hello Greta," the sergeant said to the woman he had known for over fifteen years. "Can you tell me what has happened to the lads?"

"Someone has done something to them, Adam," she cried. "And I don't know where Charles is."

The Sergeant took one look at the boy, and decided on his next course of action.

"Take the lad round to the station," he ordered. "Greta and I will go look for Charles."

The burly sergeant gently led Greta to the police car, but turned to take another look at the still sobbing boy, "Oh, and send for an ambulance. And hurry!"

"Yes sir, sergeant, sir," Fagan whispered under his breath. "Three bags, bloody full, sir," he repeated.

"Thank you," Greta said as the sergeant revved the motor up.

"Where do you think Charles is?" he asked.

"Somewhere near Ironmills Bridge, and hurry.

The car skidded around on its axis, wheels spinning, and sped off down the street.

"I suppose it's all right for sergeants to spin the bloody wheels of the police cars," Constable Fagan moaned to the boy as he half-carried him to the station.

Old mother Baxter finally closed the six inch gap in her door and locked it.

*What is the village coming to?* she thought as she hobbled down the hallway.

Then as she walked into her sitting room, she heard a noise from upstairs. She looked up to the top of her staircase and called to Oscar, her cat. Then a shadow quickly crossed her landing, and she heard the cat hiss. There was an eerie silence before she heard the cat spit and then, in a moment, there was pandemonium upstairs. Ornaments were falling, and smashing, and it sounded like her window blind was being shredded. She bravely climbed the stairs, calling the cat's name as she went. Then as she turned the corner of the landing, the noise that greeted her almost caused her to fall downstairs. She clung to the banister rail, afraid. The high pitched sound was coming from the main bedroom, where the door was fully opened. Suddenly everything fell silent, and this frightened her even more than the noise had.

The old woman moved slowly into her bedroom, through the doorway. The first thing that came into view was the cracked glass in her husband's picture frame. This was the only decent photo she had kept of him, and she picked it up from the floor. Other stuff had fallen from the dressing table, but she was unconcerned about this as she moved further into the room.

Then she fainted!

The cat was on the bed, and the large dying rat in its mouth had just given its last kick. The cat darted downstairs, over the old woman's face, the rat still held firmly in its teeth.

As Greta and the sergeant drove slowly across the bridge, Greta put her hand to her mouth and made an odd sound. She had spotted her son first, in the glare of the headlights. He was lying face down at the side of the road. The running water coming down from the high hills, lapped at his feet.

Greta was out off the car before it even came to a stop and fell to her knees in the cold water. She pulled her son upright. The lightning overhead forked across the sky and the crash of thunder that followed almost deafened them.

Charles was shaking violently, and gave out a long low moan.

"You're going to be all right, son," the sergeant said as he lifted the boy from her.

Then an ambulance appeared from nowhere, and Greta and her son were soon speeding off in it.

The large sergeant stared uneasily into the forest for a moment, as the thunder boomed overhead. Then he quickly jumped back into the police car, and sped off.

The doctor had been called to the police station, and was talking to Brian. The boy seemed to have improved somewhat.

Yet, when Brian spoke, the doctor and Constable Fagan looked at each other in disbelief.

*No*, thought the doctor. *This boy would need a different kind of help. More help than I can give him, that's for sure.*

"The Banshee," Brian cried. "It came down from the branches and held Charles tightly against a tree as it stared into his face. I swear it,"

As the speeding ambulance neared the hospital, the forked lightning speared at the road ahead of it. The frightened driver sped on.

Charles suddenly awoke, screaming. And as he tried to fight his way up from the ambulance bed, Greta and the paramedic held him down.

"Take it easy son," the paramedic said.

"Where's Brian, where's Brian?"

"Brian's all right, Charles, he's at the police station," Greta answered softly.

"Mother, it came to me from the trees. I looked into its eyes. I-I saw him!" Charles stuttered...

"What came to you son? Who did you see?" Greta asked, puzzled.

Charles stared at his mother for a moment before speaking, "It was a Banshee. It floated down from the trees to me. But when I looked into its eyes, I saw him."

"Who?" Greta asked again.

"I-I can't say," the wide eyed boy whispered.

"Tell me who you saw!" Greta shouted. She was sick and tired of their bloody, stupid mind games with her.

Charles stared to the floor, and it was a full minute before he answered her.

"Father came to me, it was father!"

Later that day, Greta stared out from the hospital window. Now she knew. Charles had never lied to her, and Ben hadn't run away. She believed now that her husband hadn't been in a fight all those years ago. The stories about the Banshee claiming its victims were true. Greta knew and believed the stories, because when she was a small girl she had witnessed one of these grotesque creatures at close hand. But it had passed her by as it swept quickly through the trees, as though she were invisible.

At the time, she couldn't understand just what she had seen. But later, she heard the stories of the beast that stalked the forest. Since that day Greta always believed she'd had a very lucky escape.

Now she knew the truth about her husband. A banshee had looked upon him, she believed, and he had left the house knowing it was going to take him. He had bravely done this so that it wouldn't come for him in front of his family, and harm them.

"Oh Ben," Greta moaned, as she stared across the rain soaked car park to the swirling trees, out passed the fields.

Something else was staring back at her as she stood at the hospital window. Out from the darkness, behind the bushes, it watched. Deep inside the hood, its mouth twitched, and formed a sort of twisted smile. Then it hissed loudly, and moved away, deeper into the trees, beyond the forest's edge.

Printed in the United Kingdom
by Lightning Source UK Ltd.
124495UK00001B/55/A